YESTERDAY IS HISTORY

YESTERDAY IS HISTORY

~~WITHDRAWN~~

KOSOKO JACKSON

sourcebooks
fire

Published by Sourcebooks Fire, an imprint of Sourcebooks
P.O. Box 4410, Naperville, Illinois 60567-4410
(630) 961-3900
sourcebooks.com

The Library of Congress Cataloging-in-Publication data is on file with the publisher.

Printed and bound in the United States of America.
LSC 10 9 8 7 6 5 4 3 2 1

To my mother, who always believed in me,
even when I didn't.

And to everyone who has ever felt lost.
You'll find your way. I promise.

On December 22, 2020, a boy just shy of twenty-two was hit by a drunk driver at 3:15 p.m., right outside of Boston, Massachusetts.

He would die forty-five minutes later, and his death would change the fate of one particular boy's life forever.

He just didn't know it.

SIX MONTHS LATER

PART ONE

ONE

"So, that went well!"

My father is always optimistic. I think it has something to do with his profession. Or maybe the way he grew up. He's one of those people who was raised to think that the world is what you make it and that people are inherently good. And because of that, he's always cheery and always able to see the bright side.

And though I love my father, his constant joy is nauseating when all I want to do is go to sleep.

"I have a good feeling about this," he says, still annoyingly optimistic.

Kill me.

I don't completely blame him. Today *is* a good day. The best we've had in a while. The doctor said my new liver seems to be adapting to me quite nicely. Like I'm some kind of adopted dog.

Except, with a dog, if something bad happens, you can return it. If we returned my liver, I'd for sure die. So it's definitely different.

I understand why he's happy. Mom, too, even though she

couldn't make it to the appointment. Hell hath no fury like a woman *this close* to getting tenure.

His joy being justified is the only reason I'm not groaning or throwing him some snide remark. Instead I'm just looking out the window, watching Boston pass us by.

"And just think, the next time you're here, it'll be for medical school—and then your residency and then your fellowship and—"

"Dad."

He raises one hand, his version of raising the white flag. "Sorry. You know how…"

"Excited you get about medicine? I know."

Not just any medicine, though—specifically, my future in medicine. A word of advice for my future self when I'm reincarnated: don't tell your parents when you're six that you want to be a doctor, because they will absolutely never let it go.

And, technically, I'm not done with the hospital yet. I'll have checkups from here to eternity. But for all intents and purposes, my life is mine again. I can just be that student with the killer college essay about how I overcame cancer and it made me stronger *and that's why I would make an excellent addition to the University of Pennsylvania community! Go Quakers!*

Take that, hepatocellular carcinoma.

"You're quieter than usual," Dad says. "You okay? Feeling queasy? Tired? Something else? How's the pain?"

"I'm fine. No. Yes. No. Pain is normal, I promise."

It's not, but *pain* isn't the right word to describe what I'm feeling. It feels like the back of a metal chair has been pressing against my stomach for too long.

"Good," Dad says, making a turn. "You'll tell me if—"

"Yes, I will."

My phone vibrates in my pocket. I twist my body and reach for it, but the movement pulls at something, and I hiss. Dad snaps his head toward me and slowly starts to move over to the shoulder, but I wave my hand, dismissing his concern. I finally grab my phone and check the screen. It's a text from my best friend Isobel.

Are you a mutant yet?

That's...not how it works.

You didn't answer the question.
Stacey thinks you'd be a good
pyrokinetic.

I knew I liked her. Keep her around. So
much better for you than Kiki.

Rude. I loved Kiki.

You LIKED Kiki. You LOVE Stacey.

"Tell Isobel I say hi," Dad says.

I text his greeting to her without looking and close my eyes, leaning back, letting the rocking of the car soothe me.

My moment of darkness and quiet only lasts half a minute before my phone vibrates again.

Tell him hi back.
Also tell him he looked hot in that pic
he posted last week.

I'm not telling my father my best friend
thinks he's hot. There must be a law
against that.

Pretty sure there isn't.

Aren't you gay, anyway?

Sexuality, just like gender, is a
construct. Don't be a prude.

Don't have the hots for my dad.

I'll consider it. If you do one thing
for me.

This sounds dangerous and like
something I'm going to regret.

It's so easy to type out the words *I'm fine*, because that's not actually a lie and doesn't make my chest feel tight with guilt. I *am* fine, in the most basic, dictionary definition of the word. I'm one of the lucky ones. Dr. Moore reminded me of that every time we came for an appointment.

The things I'm feeling—the hunger, the soreness, the mental exhaustion of listening to my parents obsess over my health—are good things. I should embrace them, not push against them.

Not everyone is as lucky as I am to have parents who can pay for a treatment that, even after insurance, cost us a fortune.

I'm lucky. Which is a weird thing to say. In most countries, my treatment would be free—or damn near free. In America, going into outrageous debt to save your life is considered "affordable care."

We're so lucky to live in the greatest country in the world.

But, right now, my focus isn't on the economics of health care but on the dull pain I've had since we left Harte Hospital.

But if I told Isobel that, she'd obsessively worry. And my father would be even worse. Besides, it's probably just a by-product of the transplant, right?

Right.

Somewhere in between the *Here & Now* and *Fresh Air* program shift on NPR, I fall asleep. I hear Dad attempt to close the door to the Prius as gently as possible, so as not to wake me. Sadly, he lacks any sort of grace.

"How did it go?" I hear Mom say.

"Well enough," he says. "Andre's tired. Which is to be expected. As long as he doesn't start vomiting, he's fine."

My phone vibrates again, so I rise and scan an unreasonable number of messages from Isobel.

[25 minutes ago]

You didn't answer me.

[22 minutes ago]

OMG, are you dead?

[17 minutes ago]

Wait, you never told me what you wanted
me to say in your eulogy if you die.

[16 minutes ago]

Can I rap? PLEASE let me rap
something.
I'm taking that as a yes. Expect some
Cardi B. Wait, you won't be able to
hear me. Shit. Damn it, Andre. Always
so f'ing selfish.

Before I can text back the perfect response, Mom knocks on the passenger's side window, waving at me.

"Dad says you're hungry. I made your favorite."

Every time I go to the hospital, Mom makes the same thing:

chicken noodle tortilla soup. It's her way of making up for not being able to come. Today, there's also the scent of homemade brownies with pecans in the air.

My mother can't bake worth shit, but now, thanks to a lie I told when I was six, this is what I have to deal with—her rock-hard brownies.

I trudge into the house, and just as I'm sitting, she says, "I threw in some protein powder too."

"I'm sorry, what?"

She puts the bowl in front of me. "For your strength. You need your energy."

"I agree, and you know how you get that? Sleep. Good food. Not—"

My phone chirps. An email from my school account. I fish out my phone and scan it. Seeing the subject line is enough to make my heart sink: RE: YOUR CLASS OF 2022 STATUS.

"Speaking of sleep, I think I'm just going to lie down for a bit," I say. "I'm just tired, guys," I quickly add, putting my hands up defensively. And I don't have the stomach to push through consuming my mom's brownies. "Long day. Being Black in America is taxing, you know." As if they wouldn't know.

The joke flies true, lodging itself in the chink in my parents' overprotective armor. Dad scoffs, Mom rolls her eyes, and they both relax. I slip upstairs.

There's nothing good in this email. I know it. Ever since being diagnosed, life at St. Clements has been hell. Not socially. Academically. The school has rigorous standards, and missing classes because of, you know, *cancer* doesn't seem to be an acceptable reason to take classes remotely.

Once my door is closed (and locked), I lean against the wall, reading the email from my guidance counselor as quickly as possible.

Dear Andre,

I hope you're doing well. I wanted to let you know that I talked to Headmistress Welchbacher, and I did my best. You won't be able to graduate with the class of 2022 unless you take the summer school classes listed below.

Please note that even if you receive a passing grade for these classes, you will not be eligible for salutatorian, as calculus, world history, and fiction writing are being offered through a community college. I have arranged a meeting with the headmistress for this upcoming Monday at 9:45 a.m. Please let me know if you're not feeling up to it, and I'll reschedule.

I hope you're feeling better.

Ms. Harper
Guidance Counselor
St. Clements Academy

I can hear my own heartbeat thumping. I can feel every red blood cell careening through my veins at what feels like hundreds of miles per hour. My palms feel warm, and my vision is black around the edges, making everything look blurry, like when a droplet of water connects with a watercolor painting.

I reread the email, hoping I missed a crucial word that will change the meaning completely.

No such luck.

Not graduating with my class, with Isobel, is a shot to the gut, but even if I *do* what they say, I still lose my salutatorian status? I worked hard for that! How many countless nights did I spend substituting books for blankets? How many weekends in the library? Parties missed? Dates turned down?

I swallow thickly, but my throat is dry and the scratchiness of it makes me wince. Dozens of questions fly through my head at a rate I can't control. What will happen to me now? Will I ever graduate? What will Mom and Dad think? They'll be beyond disappointed that their ten-year plan for me—college, medical school, the works—is being thrown out of sync.

Instead of focusing on getting better and returning to my life, I'm trying to decide how to salvage it.

"Fuck cancer."

If none of this had ever happened, I'd have a normal life. I'd be graduating next year. I'd be going to UPenn. I'd be making some piss-poor decisions with Izzy next summer. Now I'm stuck living my life on a loop.

It's like I'm being punished twice: first by the cancer and now by possibly having to repeat this year if I don't pass these classes.

I wish I could just go back in time and do it all over again.

Go back, like, three years, tell my parents to take me to the doctor, find the cancer when it's stage 0, and stop all of *this* from happening.

I put the letter down, and all I can think about is how nice my bed will feel. How my mom says a good nap always makes things look better.

She should trademark that.

When the back of my legs connect with the edge of the bed, I let gravity do the rest. All I can think of as I fall backward into my covers is how much I hope everything will be better when I wake up.

But the comforter that my head hits feels hard. Not only that, it feels wet, like...dew?

Did Clyde, our husky, pee on my bed? Again? That's the first thing that comes to mind when I fall into wet bedsheets. But it's also suddenly colder. Did Mom turn the AC up to full arctic blast, blatantly disregarding how the AC destroys our atmosphere?

But as I open my mouth to scream out the stereotypical teenage battle cry—an elongated *Mom!*—my fingers brush up against what should be a checked bedspread.

And instead, they touch grass.

Cold, wet grass.

TWO

The grass is refreshing. Slightly wet but cool. It's most definitely not my bed.

I lie there for at least five seconds, like an idiot, with my palms pressed against the soft, chilly blades, looking up at endless black sky that's replaced the ugly off-white ceiling I've stared at for almost my whole life. These five seconds are the most peaceful I've had in the past six months.

And then I realize something's wrong.

I sit up quickly and jump to my feet faster than I should. The ground rushes up and the world spins.

My eyes finally adjust to the darkness, and I'm able to come up with two possible explanations for my change in location.

One, somehow I've gotten up from bed without realizing it, and I'm standing on my street, the same street where I learned how to ride a bike and parallel park, where I almost had my first kiss, and where I broke my arm in seventh grade.

Two, somehow I've gotten up from bed without realizing it, and I'm standing in a twilight-zone version of my street.

And, shockingly, option two seems more likely, because something is really off.

Mr. Cameron's house looks...cleaner than it ever has. The blue paneling is a brighter blue than I can remember. And Ms. Cunningham's house across the street? There's no fountain there, and I know there should be, because the homeowners association had a *field day* debating whether she should be allowed to have it. And, of course, there are two cars in Mr. Evans's driveway, suspiciously retro-looking ones, when I know there should only be one, since his wife left him last year (but he doesn't want to talk about it).

But, most importantly, the house at 2405 Stuart Drive, *my* house, isn't *my* house anymore. It's *a* house, someone else's house. Someone with a penchant for wind chimes.

And...the addition is missing.

"What the actual fuck," I whisper.

The cul-de-sac is familiar, but the houses, the cars, they are all...different.

"Okay, okay, Andre," I tell myself quickly. "Deep breaths, that's it. Breathe. You know how to do that. Breathing still makes sense, right?"

But my breaths come out shallow, despite how hard I try to breathe in for five seconds, hold for three, and breathe out for seven. I read that somewhere. But it feels like I can't get enough air, no matter how hard I try. Like I'm actually suffocating on oxygen. If that's even *possible*.

Catastrophizing won't solve anything! I scold myself mentally, the voice in my head barely breaking through the sound of blood pumping in my ears. I rub my palms together, feeling the rough grains of dirt, the dew, and the sharp grass sticking to my palms. It feels so real.

But no matter how real it feels, it can't be real. That's what happens when you have two parents who swear up and down by the scientific method. It rubs off on you.

"Sleepwalking...or dreaming," I reason, dusting off my jeans. That's something I can wrap my head around. Maybe hallucinations are a side effect of the antirejection meds.

Reaching back, I gingerly touch the back of my head, which hit the ground hard when I fell, and wince, feeling around the inflamed skin, checking my fingers.

No blood. Good.

Or bad?

Is this what being in a coma is like? Had I drifted off to sleep and something went completely wrong, and now I'm in the hospital, hooked up to dozens of tubes, fighting for my life while my mom and dad decide to keep me on or take me off life support?

Oh God.

Oh God.

Oh God.

"Uh, hey?" a voice says to the left of me. I see him in my peripheral vision, waving at me as he walks around the front of a white car that's just cruised into the driveway.

He's dressed in a normal outfit: a white undershirt with a pair of jeans and boots. It's a simple look, and he wears it well.

His shaggy blond hair falls over his bright blue eyes, and he brushes it back in a nonchalant way that tells me he does this maybe a dozen times a day.

But something feels…off.

"You lost?" he asks, throwing his leather jacket over his shoulder like he's a half-price James Dean.

How do I answer that? Honestly? Because that answer would be: *Yes. I'm completely freakin' lost.*

But instead, I turn back to the house, willing it to look familiar. Hoping I'll wake up from whatever bizarro dream this is.

But nothing happens.

I turn back to the stranger and open my mouth, close it, and open it again. He simply grins, his arms now crossed over his chest, waiting patiently with an open, if slightly confused, smile on his face.

"Where am I?"

"You took all that time to think up something to say, and that's what you settle on?" He shakes his head and grins. "Boston, Massachusetts."

He's from around here, I think. Says it like all other natives. *Baws-ton.* Good. That's at least something I can work with.

In my journalism elective, I was told that the easiest questions are usually the simplest ones, and the simplest ones will get you all you need to know—if you know how to ask them and how to read between the lines. I know the where.

"Are you lost?" he asks again.

"No, I'm from around here too."

"Which part?"

"H—" Nope, can't say that. "Nearby. I must have gotten off at the wrong station. Can you point me to Forest Hills?"

He frowns. He has an expressive face. You can see every emotion on it. I guess he can't help wearing his heart on his sleeve.

"Forest Hills? The Orange Line?" I ask.

"I know what you mean. Just never heard someone ask me that before. Odd question. Hard to spot and all," he says with a sarcastic tone.

"Sorry?"

A heavy awkwardness appears between us as suddenly as a spring shower. His face twists into a confused expression, a mix of *Is this boy dangerous?* and *What is he talking about?*

But he speaks softly, not like he's scared, like he's concerned. "You okay, boss?"

I should just say yes and walk away—in any direction. I should say goodbye, thank him, and move on.

But I never do things the easy way. At my core, I'm a problem solver. And this is a problem worth solving.

The boy points in the general direction that I need.

"Thanks," I reply, taking a few steps before pausing and turning to him. But I stop. I need to know something first.

"What did you mean my question was odd?"

"First you don't know where one of the ugliest T stops is, and now you're asking me an obvious question," he teases. "You sure you're okay?"

"I'm fine." Which is a lie, but he doesn't need to know that.

I employ a tactic my mom uses—silence. Eventually, he'll get uncomfortable and answer. *In three, two, one...*

"T stops are easy to spot," he caves, fishing out a cigarette and lighter. "I mean, they're aboveground, loud, ugly as shit, and—"

Hold up. "Stop," I interrupt. "You said its *above*ground?"

"Mm-hmm." He lights the thin white cancer stick in two clicks.

"Forest Hills is underground."

"Underground?" he repeats, voice muffled with the cig in his mouth. He pulls it out, holding it between two long fingers. "That would be something, wouldn't it? No. Pretty sure I know my stations."

"Me too."

Silence again, except this time it's not my doing. He narrows his eyes curiously, scanning me, it feels like, for information.

"You sure you okay, boss?"

"*I'm fine*," I repeat. Why is this guy saying the station is aboveground? What a stupid thing to lie about. It's something I can confirm easily, and—

Wait.

Wait.

Then, like when a random song lyric from years ago suddenly pops into your head, memories from viewing old photos during middle school history class flood my brain. Black-and-white photos, and photos with poor color quality of Boston. The *old* Boston. Boston in the 1950s and 1960s.

With aboveground trains.

"When is it?" I suddenly ask. "Still summer?"

He nods, but slower this time, his eyes studying me. "June, actually."

"June fourteenth?"

"Right on the money."

"And what year is it? Two thousand twenty-one, right?"

A beat passes, and it's the longest beat of my life.

"Right?"

He looks concerned, very concerned, but he answers. Not the answer I want to hear, though. Not the answer anyone wants to hear.

"Nineteen sixty-nine."

The words echo and bounce around my brain for what feels like hours before they finally lodge themselves into my psyche.

I'm back on my ass before I even realize it, my legs buckling under me.

He moves forward and, ignoring the wetness of the grass, falls to his knees beside me. He presses the back of his hand against my forehead.

"You're warm. Are you sick or something? Confused?"

"I'm okay." I bat his hand away. "I just need...some..."

"You need some water. You're coming with me."

He counts to three before hoisting me up, slinging my left arm over his shoulder.

"I can walk."

"Don't worry, I won't tell anybody." He winks, walking

across the lawn to the front steps. "Stand here for a sec," he says, fishing out his keys. He keeps me close, even though I'm perfectly capable of standing on my own.

I'm not sure I mind it.

He turns the key and uses his shoulder and a little extra effort to push the door open, stumbles when it gives, and gives me a boyish smile.

"Always gets stuck…"

"When it rains," I finish the sentence for him. I remember that when my parents bought the house, they complained about it. The doors were one of the first things we changed… But sometimes they still get stuck.

He looks puzzled but shrugs it off and walks into his house.

My house.

Fifty-two years in the past.

THREE

My parents bought this house after it had been abandoned for more than fifteen years.

I was six when we moved in. My mom taught me how to remember where we lived with a little memory trick.

"We're next to the Forest Hills T stop, and Forrest is your middle name, but with two *r*s."

Many of the changes Mom and Dad made when we renovated it erased the old house. But some things are still here. Like the slight dip you have to walk over when you move from the front hallway to the living room. Or the strange half-foot extension that makes passing through the living room and into the kitchen not as seamless as it should be. I know it so well, inside and out. At its core, this is still my house.

The guy weaves through the house with an uncanny familiarity that feels…violating. It takes me a few moments of silence to figure out why.

It's because I move the same way when I'm home. It's the same level of relaxation, of comfort that comes from being in your own home. It's the way your muscles relax and that breath you've been holding without knowing it is finally released when you get home. It's the subconscious feeling of safety. He has it. And I don't right now, but then again, I think I'm losing my mind. How can it be 1969? The only logical explanation is that it's a dream…or a hallucination. I'm trying not to freak out—trying to ride out whatever this is, but I can feel the bile rising in the back of my throat as I try to fight down the panic.

"So we have water, pop, Tang…" He lists off drinks, his body half concealed by the fridge. He doesn't tell me to sit, but I lean against a bar stool, resting my arms on the cool countertop. Why is he so calm when he clearly has a lunatic in his house?

"No one here calls it pop."

"That's because you're all wrong," he says, without looking up. "Which do you want?"

Instead of answering him, I take everything in. From the corner of my eye, I see him looking at me.

"You look like you need something stronger. Sidecar? Sidecar."

"Sure, whatever."

We are both silent while he makes the drink. I get off the stool and walk over to the hearth. There's no fireplace in my house anymore, just a wall where the TV hangs. But the pictures on the mantel are cute. The guy with his family—an older brother, two parents, a dog—except they all look younger. Especially him.

"An all-American family," I mutter. "Did I end up in *Leave It to Beaver*? All you're missing is the white picket fence."

"Sorry?"

"Nothing," I say, looking up, seeing him pour the drinks. "Andre," I blurt out. "Andre Cobb."

"Hmm?"

"My name."

"Nice to meet you Andre Cobb from Boston," he teases. "I'm Michael. Michael Gray, since we're giving our full government names."

With drinks in hand, Michael pads across the floor, handing a martini glass filled with orangeish liquid to me. The proportions are off; mine has about a third more liquid than his. He grins sheepishly.

"I'm still getting the hang of this stuff," he admits. The hesitation on my face as he raises his glass in a silent salute makes him pause. "Not a fan of orange liquor? Look, I get it. Took me a while to get used to it, too, but I promise it's amazing."

I push my lips into a thin line to keep the secret from escaping accidentally. What do I tell him? That I've never drunk alcohol before? That starting now, right after my transplant, probably isn't the best time to do it? But if it'll calm my nerves so that I can control them enough to ride this thing out…

"Cheers."

The drink goes down smoothly, once I get past the initial burn. The sugary sweetness helps, and within three gulps, my drink is almost gone, while he's already refilled his halfway.

Michael rubs at his bottom lip with his thumb in a slow-motion move that I'm one hundred percent sure he didn't mean to be seductive but one hundred percent is. He then shakes his head, blowing air out of his lips obnoxiously.

"Note to self: I hate cognac," Michael says, putting the glass down.

Why did he invite me in? I'm a mess. I'm spouting nonsense about the future. Maybe Michael is just a super friendly type of guy. Or he just isn't scared.

For the millionth time, I think this has to be an illusion or a dream or something.

But it feels so real. The smell of disinfectant lingers softly in the air, but it's there. The house doesn't have a speck of dust in it; it feels like some old-timey replica made for a museum to show what life was like in the sixties.

"Shit," I say, seeing the tracks of mud from my shoes. "I should have taken these off."

Michael waves his hand dismissively. "Don't sweat it. You're lucky. Parents and brother are out of town for the week."

"And the dog too?"

Michael smirks. "That tells you where I rank in the family dynamics, yeah? I'll clean it myself—or just take the blame myself. They'll accept that." He nods his head toward the picture I was looking at before. "Screwup Mikey. That's what my pops calls me. This will be par for the course. You said you're looking for the Orange Line, right? Shame, really. I'm going to miss you when you're gone."

"Yeah, I am. Wait, pause and go back. What do you mean when I'm gone?"

Michael quirks his brow. "You plan on staying forever? Well, trust me, you're very fetching and all, but I don't think my parents would be very happy with me having a boy or a Neg—"

"Don't you dare finish that sentence."

He pauses, studies my seriousness, and slowly nods. "A stranger in the house with me. But they won't be home till tomorrow. So we got time."

"Time for what?"

Michael smiles, the same one as before. He walks over to the couch and plops down, putting his booted feet on the table, crossing them at the ankles. "Time for me to figure you out."

Before I can respond, he speaks again. "You're from around here, yeah?"

"Mm-hmm."

With him sitting, I have the advantage if I need to run. I'm not giving that up. I've seen what happens in those science-fiction shows when people are stuck inside their mind and try to leave. This house is probably some metaphor for me being trapped inside my consciousness. I bet if I leave the cul-de-sac, there will be nothingness until I need there to be something.

"But I have no idea where you're trying to go…hmm. What a puzzle you are, Andre," he muses. "You smoke?"

I shake my head this time. Michael shrugs. "I should quit. You know smoking causes cancer? That's what they're saying. Not sure if I believe them."

How could he not *believe* them? There're layers upon layers of proof.

"I would one hundred percent agree with that choice."

Michael smiles, showing off a row of perfectly straight white teeth. He rests his arms on the back of the couch, his shirt riding up slightly, revealing a tight set of abs with a light dusting of dirty blond hair. He's relaxed, in his element.

I, on the other hand, haven't been this tense since Dr. Moore told me I was sick.

"So here's the way I look at it, Andre," Michael finally says. "You have nowhere to go. And where you want to go, I can't help you. You can go out there, into Boston at night, and try to find it on your own. But you seem like a smart cat, and for someone like you"—he gestures—"it wouldn't be wise to be wandering around Boston in the dark alone."

"Someone like me?"

"You know what I mean."

Of course I do. It's the same thing my mom would say. Boston hasn't always been great for Black people—for anyone who isn't white, really. Sure, it's better now, a lot better, but there's a chance that this is real. And if it's real, I'm not in my timeline anymore. There's a chance...a chance I've *actually* traveled back in time.

And no matter how slim that chance is, I'm safer here. In Michael's house...my house.

"And I think you are a little messed up," Michael says. "Don't even know what year it is. So what I'm suggesting is that you stay here the night. Until the morning. And we just hang out…talk."

"Wait," I say. "Talk?"

Michael leans forward, resting his elbows on his knees. "Is that something you don't do?"

"Cut the crap. Someone just randomly appears in your lawn, someone who seems to be very confused, and your first idea is to bring him in, serve him alcohol, offer him your couch, and *talk* to him?"

He shrugs. "Is that such a bad thing?"

"It's weird."

"Some people would say it's the responsible and neighborly thing to do."

"Some people are wrong."

"Or maybe I'm just a nice person."

"Or maybe you're an idiot for letting a stranger into your home."

Another shrug. "The way I see it, there are two options here. One, you're someone who needs my help."

"And the second option?" I cross my arms and examine him. There are no telltale signs of him lying. But who can really be that selfless? He should be afraid. He should be calling the police. Hell, that's what I would do—that's what *most* people would do.

"I was hoping you could help me with that one."

"I'm sorry?"

He takes another sip of his drink, a longer one. The ice cubes clink against one another. His Adam's apple bobs, and his collarbone flexes just slightly while he sips. Michael's defined enough that even small actions like that have visible effects, and I'd be lying if I said they weren't nice to look at. The whole "jeans and T-shirt" look really does suit him.

Michael stands up and takes one step forward. I take one step back. The tango continues until my back presses against the wall and he's less than three inches away from me. I can smell the soft scent of alcohol and lemon on his breath. I take a deep breath, though I don't mean to; the smell just does that to me. Dad told me once that smell is the sense most tied to memories and emotions.

I believe it.

Michael puts one hand on the wall next to me. "You're a smart guy, Andre."

"I know that."

He smiles, but gently. "Didn't mean it as an insult. Or a compliment. Only saying the truth. And what I know about smart guys is, they're the ones you gotta watch out for. The ones who always have a secret. I'd know, because I'm a smart guy too."

Even though we've only spent fifteen minutes together, I know that Michael knows the effect he has on people. He *revels* in it.

That is the most dangerous type of boy.

"I'm not hiding anything." I force the words out. They feel like lead in my mouth. I can feel my chest vibrating as my heart beats faster and faster.

"But you're debating if a T stop is aboveground or underground, asking me what year it is, you're dressed funny, and, to top it off, you don't carry yourself like anyone I've ever seen before. You're definitely hiding something."

There could be millions of reasons why I'm seeing and experiencing what I am. Maybe I'm on the verge of death, and my neurons are firing to create one great memory.

So many maybes. But deep down, I know what I want to say; I know what I'm feeling and thinking.

"I'm either dreaming or hallucinating...but if this is real, I think I traveled back in time and ended up in my own house in nineteen sixty-nine."

There, I think. *I said it.* Speaking the words feels like pressure on a dam being released at the very last minute. Sure, it sounds like nonsense, and sure, Michael's probably going to tackle me, tie me to the couch, and call 911. *Hello, Operator? Yeah, I have a stranger in my house who says he's from the future. Sure, I'll hold.* But at least I said it.

"You asked earlier if the year was 2021. Is that when you're from?"

That wasn't what I expected. That wasn't what I expected at all.

I open my mouth to answer him, and the world around me starts to blur, starting with the corners of my eyes. The ground under me feels like it's suddenly gone, and I'm falling but also rising at the same time. It's like what I imagine being in a black hole feels like: being yanked and turned into a thin piece of spaghetti.

And then, it all happens in reverse. My body retracts, sounds become crisp, colors return, and I feel something...wet?

The rough, sticky dampness is a familiar feeling. The stench of wet dog.

I open my eyes to see Clyde's brown, wide ones looking up at me, his front paws on my thighs, licking at my stomach through my shirt.

I instantly jump back, like Clyde is some foreign intruder. It takes me a moment to see everything—to really *see* everything around me. My bed. The messy room. The papers. My cell phone.

This is my room. This is my home. Well, my home in my time. Not...then.

I gasp. "I'm back."

FOUR

"Andre! Breakfast!"

I've been lying in bed all night, just staring at my familiar ceiling. It's my room, all right. Down to the clothes, the smell, the books. But I have to keep double-checking and confirming. Touching the books, feeling the bed, calling Clyde over, and examining every inch of him before it sets in.

Finally, I sit up. Three things run through my mind at the same time, but I do my best to order them. I'm a scientist-in-training, like my dad always says—no matter how much it annoys me—so it's time I think like one.

One, I'm alive. That's clear, and it's a good first step.

Two, my vitals are fine—pulse is rapid (but that's to be expected), no wounds, my scar looks the same, completely healed. I even pinch myself to make sure it's real. Get rid of all shadows of doubt.

Three, I need to analyze what could have caused this. Could it have been a hallucination? Maybe, but it felt too real. A side effect of medication? Perhaps, but I did my research—so did Mom and Dad—and none of the drugs had these types of effects. Was it a dream? Why did I remember it so vividly if it was? Could I be having a mental breakdown? Possibly.

Or, it could be the fifth option: I just freakin' *time traveled*.

"Andre!"

I press my feet against the floor tentatively. This is definitely my reality. This is my world, and for right now, that's all that matters.

Mom and Dad are at the breakfast table when I finally make it down. Cinnamon rolls, freshly squeezed orange juice, and half a dozen other treats decorate the table.

"Are you practicing for Thanksgiving already?" I ask, teasing. Mom rolls her eyes, but she has a bashful expression on her face.

"I told her not to cook so much," Dad says, ribbing her. "We're not going to eat all this."

"Hush," she scolds him. "Your son got a clean bill of health. He's a cancer survivor. That's big. The least we can do is—"

"Give him diabetes?" Dad interrupts, poking a pancake with a fork. "How much syrup did you..."

Mom gives him *that look*. We both know the look, and he shuts up. Dad does his best, bless his heart, to eat healthily and to instill those values in us. Mom and I are just too addicted to sugar.

"Thanks...it's...perfect?" And I mean it, which is a surprise. The pancakes are, shockingly, perfectly fluffy. The cinnamon rolls have the perfect amount of warmth and gooey sugar.

And the fruit? Fresh and in season. And for the first time in a very long time, I feel...hungry.

She's been practicing, I think. *Probably for this exact moment when I came home with a clean bill of health.*

Mom beams with pride at her meal. "You're surprised, aren't you?"

I nod, my mouth full of food.

"It is pretty perfect, right?" she says. "Your old mom has some tricks still."

"You're most definitely not old."

"You're just saying that because you're my son."

"And because it's the truth!"

Mom gives me a skeptical look, but Dad clears his throat, breaking the moment.

"So," Dad says after a moment. "How are you feeling? Heard you tossing and turning last night."

Thank God that's all they heard, I think.

"Couldn't sleep."

"Are you hurting?" Mom asks.

"No, I'm fine."

"Is your pain gone?"

"You mean the pain I told you wasn't a problem yesterday?"

Dad doesn't reply. He knows that I know what he's talking about.

"Yes, Dad."

"What pain?" Mom asks.

"It was nothing."

"It was something," Dad interjects.

"Maybe we should call Dr. Moore?" Mom suggests.

"Might be a good idea," Dad agrees and pulls out his phone. "I'm sure she can fit us in."

"I said I'm fine, guys, really."

A phone vibrates softly.

"What's your schedule like today?" Mom asks Dad.

"I have a class to teach, but I can get the TA to do it. You?"

"A thesis defense, but that's in the morning. Can you do the afternoon?"

"Morning is better for me. I need to attend a funding meeting across town for the new lab."

The vibration hums again. It takes me one more vibration to realize that it's coming from my phone.

The area code is 617. That's Boston. But it's not a Boston number I know. Curious, I answer.

"Hello?"

"Andre?" asks a female voice on the other end of the phone. "Andre Cobb?"

"Speaking." I stand up and walk into the adjoining living room. Mom and Dad continue arguing over schedules.

"Claire, Claire McIntyre," she says, as if I'm supposed to know that name. The silent pause I give tells her I don't.

"Of course," she says to herself and sighs. "I'm the mother of the boy who gave you your liver. Think you have time to chat?"

The words feel like a punch in the gut—a sucker punch. I remember what Dr. Moore said when we got the donor liver. *It's a perfect match*, she had said hurriedly on the speakerphone. *Poor boy died in a car accident, but his liver is intact. Get here now.*

It was a whirlwind experience. We got to the hospital at 5:30 p.m., and I had a new liver by the next morning. Dr. Moore kept saying how lucky I was, how generous the family was. How they wanted to remain anonymous.

And here the mother, or a woman claiming to be the mother of the donor, is calling me.

"Something tells me, Mrs. McIntyre, I'm going to want to hear what you have to say."

She chuckles. "You're as smart as I thought you'd be. Can you make it downtown tonight?"

"I'll be there."

FIVE

It's rare to see Isobel Powell-Ito pouting.

It's a specific look too. Lips pursed, eyes narrowed almost serpentlike, and her hands clenched into fists. I've only seen it twice in the eight years I've known her. Once when her parents promised her a new dress and backed out at the last minute. And the other time when she was bidding for an elective at St. Clements and they said she'd won the lottery, but she actually hadn't.

But when I tell her we're not going to Back Bay for our favorite pastime, pretending to be rich and going to different art galleries, she pouts. Hard.

"You're going to get us killed, Dre."

"No one is going to be murdering anyone."

"You're going to a person's house just because they called you? That's peak killer vibes."

"It's the donor's family," I remind her. "They aren't going to kill me. They *gave* me the organ."

"So they are going to kill you to take it back," she hisses.

"Did you ever think about why they suddenly want to meet now? Maybe it's not even them! This could all be a lie!"

I can't tell her what I think it means or why I really want to go visit the McIntyres. She'll definitely think I'm losing my grip. And she might not be wrong.

Plus, if this is all a mistake, like Isobel thinks it is, I want to be able to do the normal thing: thank them for offering their son's liver to me. That's the least I can do, right? And if it's some deranged stalker lying to me about being the donor's family? Well, then I'm probably screwed anyway.

At least, that's what I tell myself.

I look out the window, watching as the streets shift from residential to city landscape to the upper echelon of Boston society. The sun set not that long ago, so the city has a haunting summertime glow about it that I love. There's nothing like Boston at dusk. The way the last light lingers over the Charles River. The only thing better is when it rains, and the cobblestone sidewalks have a silvery light to them.

"I just want to talk to them."

"Let the record show that I think this is a bad idea," she mutters, leaning over the steering wheel. We're close.

"There. At the end of the street."

Just ahead is a pristine-looking brownstone, with a gate and manicured lawn. It's three floors, and the lights are all on. There's a garage to the left of it, separated by an automatic gate. The house is wider than others on the street and takes up the space of two lots, making it almost as big as some houses I've seen in the suburbs.

"How much do you think this costs?" Isobel asks after she parks, the car rumbling before falling still.

"Ten? Twelve million?"

"Fifteen," she corrects me, holding up her phone to show me the house on Zillow. "Fifteen freakin' million, Dre. These aren't just creeps. They're rich creeps, and that's the worst type of person."

"Then you can stay in the car."

I get out of the Scion before Isobel can say anything, knowing that she'll follow me. Before I reach the gate, she's next to me, adjusting her sundress and glaring.

"I'm going to kill you if they don't do it first," she whispers, matching my pace as we approach the door. "This is why people of color die first in horror movies."

"No, that's because they make stupid choices."

"*What do you call this?*"

I turn to answer, but before I can, the oak door suddenly opens. Standing there in front of us is a woman, tall with angled, sharp cheeks. Her very ginger hair is cut in a fashionable, if not severe bob, and she's casually dressed in a Harvard T-shirt and a pair of jeans. Her wide smile is a comfort to see, given the circumstance.

She looks down at the watch on her right wrist. "Perfect timing."

"For?" Isobel asks.

Mrs. McIntyre looks at her for a moment, scanning her the way I imagine a robot would—wide green eyes moving methodically.

"I'm sorry, Miss…"

"Powell-Ito. But most people call me Isobel."

"Isobel, then. I wanted to speak to Andre alone, if possible."

"Sorry." Isobel shakes her head. "We're a package deal."

Mrs. McIntyre shakes *her* head. "I don't mean to be rude. But this is a personal matter, and it really only concerns Andre and me. You could sit in the study while he and I talk?"

"What concerns Andre concerns me."

"Apologies, Mrs. McIntyre, she's just trying to support me."

Mrs. McIntyre turns, the sharpness of her features softening to a warm grin. "Call me Claire. But I'm afraid this is…how do I put it…" Claire pauses and looks up, as if the answer might be on the roof.

There's no way I'm going to get what I need out of Claire with Isobel here. This isn't her story. This isn't her liver.

"Give us five minutes," I tell her. I don't look directly at her.

"Excuse me?"

"Give me five minutes. Any longer, and you can come inside. Is that fair?"

"Make it ten, and we have a deal," Claire says, bargaining.

"Deal," I say before Isobel can argue. This time, I turn to her. "Look, I can't explain it to you, but you have to trust me, okay? I've got this, and like we both said: ten minutes, and then you can come in."

She doesn't trust me. No, it's not that she doesn't trust

me—she doesn't trust Claire. Isobel has always been over-protective, and ever since the diagnosis…she's been even more so. A real ride-or-die friend.

"Fine. Ten minutes." She caves, turning to me. "If you need me before then, for anything, I'll be in the car."

"I said I'll be okay, Izzy." I smile to reassure her.

Isobel stares at me, and then at Claire, before turning swiftly on her heels, heading down the steps. Claire leads me inside, closing the door behind me.

The McIntyre home is the type of home you'd expect from a rich family. Everything is made of polished cherry wood, with the most advanced technology. As we walk past the living room, I see a seventy-inch TV, hundreds of books, Alexa devices in almost every room, paintings that I know are worth thousands, and family portraits of a happy all-American family, with a mother, a father, a redheaded older son, and a brown-haired younger one.

It's too perfect, honestly.

But Claire doesn't stop walking, and I appreciate that, because if we keep walking, keep moving, nothing about how weird this all is can set in, seep into my bones, and paralyze me.

"She's a fiery one, isn't she?" Claire asks.

"Isobel's protective of me."

"I'm glad you have someone like that." She leaves it at that. At the end of the hallway, there's a pair of double sliding doors, in the same wooden pattern as the floor. Behind it, muffled, I can hear a voice. It sounds like a man.

My heart races. Was Isobel right? Not only do I think about how she would never let me live it down but I also flash to my parents. I lied to them about where Isobel and I were going tonight. It came out before I could process it, and there was no going back. They think we're seeing a movie and getting dinner, and they were eager to let me have some fun—especially with someone they trusted.

But now, I'm thinking that might have been a mistake.

Claire opens the sliding doors, and they glide smoothly without a sound. Inside is their dining room, which is as big as my kitchen, living room, and foyer combined. Three large windows take over the right wall, with a table that seats at least ten people in the middle. But only one man sits at it.

"Greg, Andre. Andre, Greg. My husband."

Greg smiles broadly, a warmer grin than Claire's. It reminds me of my father: welcoming, calming, and friendly.

"Nice to meet you, Andre. Take a seat, we have plenty."

Of course: a dad joke.

"Nice to meet you both," I say. And I mean it. My parents taught me manners, after all. But they also told me to be confident. So I don't sit. Because Isobel is right. If these people really are crazy? Sitting is not where I want to be.

"First of all, I want to thank you and your son for saving my life. Truly. I wouldn't be where I am without you both. Without…your son."

How do you talk about someone in the past tense when it's so clear that he's still a part of their lives? Neither of them falter, except for Greg's eyes flicking to the photos on the walls and mantel and Claire's cheek twitching just slightly.

"I know there are a lot of people you could have given the liver to." I also know I wasn't on the top of the list, but that's a different question for another day. "I'm not sure how you found out that I was the one who got your son's organ but—"

"But do you really care?"

There's no proper way to answer that question. I settle on saying, "I care because I'm curious."

The twitch on Claire's face turns into a soft grin. There's sadness behind her eyes, but she's trained herself to smile to hide it. It's probably some sort of defense mechanism; women in power can't show weakness, but a smile? That's disarming.

"Right answer." A beat passes. "David, our son, would be happy to help, Andre."

Greg nods. "That's the type of person he was. Always helping others. Using your life to help another? This is the ultimate way of helping someone, I feel. Kinda like a coup de grâce." He laughs. If Claire's smile is her defense, then Greg's laugh is his.

"And second of all?" Claire asks.

"Sorry?"

"If there's a first of all, Andre, there has to be a second of all. You're smart, trust me, I know. You're not just smart—you're smart with a capital *S*. So what else would you like to say?"

I stand quietly, listening to the heavy beating of my heart fill my ears. It's a hard feeling to wrap your head around, knowing that you're in over your head. Claire is right. I am *Smart*.

Smart enough to know how to navigate around conversations. It's a skill my parents taught me: always have an out. Always leave a good impression.

But right here? I'm out of my depth. Claire is calm and collected. Greg is disarming and supportive. They play off each other in a synergistic way. They fit together, slotting into each other, like a true power couple, forming an impenetrable wall.

The only way out is through. And the best way through something is the truth.

"Why am I here?"

"There it is," Claire says. Greg smiles, that proud fatherly smile men give that makes me feel uncomfortable but also like I should be proud of myself.

"Long story. Should you tell him, or should I?" he asks.

"You've had a rough week, dear. I think you should. A little joy to add to an otherwise gloomy day."

"And that's why I love you so much. But this was all your idea. I think you should see it through to the end."

"And that's why I love you," she responds, kissing Greg's cheek quickly.

Claire sighs in an exasperated way that shows she's conceding, even though she has more fight in her.

"Right, then. Ripping off the Band-Aid fast is usually best," she says. "A little less than twenty-four hours ago, you did something extraordinary. Something that you might not understand, that you might want to think was a dream, or frankly, that you can't explain. I'm here to tell you that what happened to you actually did happen. You did jump through time, and you are, for all intents and purposes, a time traveler. And I know that because—"

"Because we're time travelers too!" Greg interrupts.

"Christ! Greg! You couldn't let me finish!"

Greg holds his hands up. "Sorry, sorry…"

I really did time travel. This is really happening.

SIX

I come from a family of scientists. My grandmother on my father's side was the first African American woman to graduate from Emory's medical school, and my great-grandfather on my mother's side helped the Americans on their failed attempt at cracking the Enigma code, though he was very far down the ladder and barely had any responsibility, because, you know, he was Black.

We are a family of doers. Solvers. Creators. And every solution or creation always begins the same way: eliminating any answer that doesn't make sense. It's the basis of science. I think.

"Time travel doesn't exist."

Did I want it to be real? No. In what world would time travel being a thing make *anything* easier?

My mind's racing with millions of thoughts.

"Reasonable reaction, all things considered," Greg muses. "At least he didn't run out of the room screaming."

The only reason I haven't is because what they are suggesting may be ridiculous, but there's a part of me that wants to believe it. That's staying here because maybe, just maybe, they can give me some piece of proof that will make the impossible possible.

"Why do you say that, Andre?" asks Claire.

"That time travel doesn't exist?"

She nods. "Because society tells you so? Because that's what you've been taught? What about '*i* before *e* except after *c*'? We learn when we're older that's not true all the time."

"You're comparing jumping through time and space to a bad grammatical rule?"

"Got you there, honey," Greg chimes in. "Smart and quick-witted."

"And a talented jumper," she says, still looking at me. "You've had, what, six months since the liver transplant, and you've already made your first jump?"

My body freezes. It's like in those horror movies when the character realizes that *the call is coming from inside the house*. This family knows more about me than I know about them, and that disadvantage isn't comforting.

"Why don't we start from the beginning?" I suggest. "And only honest answers."

Claire chuckles. "By the time we're done, you're going to be thinking very differently about that word."

"Start?"

"Beginning."

I push past the sense of wonder and hold my ground. It won't be long before Isobel comes bursting in, anyway.

"How do you know so much about me?"

"Money," she says bluntly, gesturing to the house. "We're rich, Andre. You're smart enough to know that the world works differently for certain people. If you're rich, you can get away with more."

"Like finding out who received a donated organ."

She smiles. "Precisely. But that was more self-preservation. No. Protection. That's a better word. We couldn't have someone jumping through time, someone who got that ability through us, walking around the world unchecked. It was as much for your protection as it was for ours."

Without another word or a request to follow her, she turns and walks back down the hall and into the study, and I obediently trail behind her.

Humming under her breath, she scans half a dozen bookshelves with her fingers before grabbing an older-looking book. She then sits on the couch and gestures for me to sit next to her. I hesitate but obey.

"For me to be honest with you, and for you to understand, you're going to have to suspend your disbelief for a few minutes," she says, dusting off the leather binding. "You're going to have to go into this believing that there is a chance that I'm telling you the truth, that time travel exists. Can you do that, Andre?"

"As long as you're honest with me, then sure."

She grins, sitting back next to me.

I move half a foot away. But she doesn't seem to mind.

"My family, and other families like us, are time travelers. It's a genetic thing, and I'm not sure when it started or how. But for as long as I can remember, people in my family have been able to do it. Jump through time and space."

She opens the book, which I realize is actually a photo album. The page she turns to is filled with four or five photos. One of them stands out. It's of the Crispus Attucks Monument designed by Robert Kraus. But in this picture, it's only half finished. I used to love that monument when I was little. Mom took me to it hundreds of times. I did over a dozen projects on Crispus Attucks, the first American, a Black man, killed at the start of the American Revolution. I know his story like the back of my hand.

I also know that the monument was erected in 1888. There is a woman in the picture, standing off to the side, a woman who looks exactly like Claire McIntyre.

I bring the photo close to my face, as if examining the grainy and slightly blurry photograph with crinkly, yellowed edges will help me make sense of what I'm seeing. The album is filled with photographs—some labeled *Statue of Liberty, 1895* and others, *The Battle of South Mountain, 1862* and *Live Aid Concert, 1985*.

And Claire is clearly there in all of them.

I close the heavy book with a loud thump, pushing it back toward her like it's some sort of cursed tome. She takes it carefully, holding the book preciously close to her chest before putting it by her side.

"Questions?"

"Many." A beat passes. "These could be photoshopped."

Claire shrugs. "They could be. Do you think they are?"

I can't say that I do, and I think that's what scares me.

"That's typical, you know. All the questions you have—logical solutions trying their best to make themselves known, to make sense of what's happening. At least, I assume that's typical. Most time travelers come from families who can perform the act. They just inherently know that this is real because it's part of their reality. It's rare for someone to just"—she snaps—"start doing it without some warning signs beforehand. It's a genetic gift, you know, and you've been lucky enough to have received it."

"I'd argue it's a curse."

For the first time since I arrived, it's her turn to look off-balance.

"And why would you say that?"

"Secrets make you lonely. They isolate you. And a secret like this, if it's actually true? That's something you can't ever afford to let loose. That's a sad way to live. Especially when you have the power to play God but, I'm assuming, can't."

"Assuming that time travel is real, of course."

"Of course."

"You're smart, Andre."

"I know."

"But in this case, you're wrong. To not be anchored to a specific time? To see the world in a way that no one else can? That's a gift that few people can experience. And you, Andre, are lucky enough now to be able to experience it."

I play along. Not because I'm worried about my safety. Because I'm curious.

"Nothing in this life is just given. It's not just the luck of the draw. Everything comes at a price and a consequence," I say.

"Spoken like someone who has never just enjoyed life for what it has to offer."

I point to my dark-skinned arm. "This doesn't allow me that."

She pauses. She swallows, her sharp collarbone becoming more pronounced as her body tenses.

"I didn't mean it like that," she says, backtracking.

"I know. No one ever does."

I breathe in and count to five. It shouldn't be my job to make her more comfortable with discussing race. I'm not a teachable moment. But that's always how this goes. Most race conversations end like this. Uncomfortable, awkward sessions of me trying to make someone else feel better. I should be used to it. I *should* be...

The front door opens suddenly, with enough force to make the photos on the wall vibrate. At first, I think it's Isobel. I'm sure it's been more than ten minutes, or close to it. But the voice that follows is deep, and the footsteps that thump against the floor are heavy.

"Hey, Mom. There's some girl sitting in the driveway glar—"

We turn to the doorway, but I'm the only one who stands. Fast enough, I might add, that the ground comes rushing up to me in a wave of dizziness. Standing there, in the flesh, is the same boy, now at least a decade older than he is in the photos. I assume he's the McIntyres' youngest son. His brown hair is matted to his forehead, and there's a sheen of sweat on him. He holds a lacrosse stick in one hand and an equipment bag in the other, and his shirt reads THE HUTCHERSON SCHOOL. My rival school.

"Blake," she says sternly. "You know I told you no cleats in the house. And you're late. I told you to be here—"

"You brought *him* here?" he interrupts.

Blake never stops looking at me. No, *looking* isn't the right word; he's staring—like his eyes are trying to bore a hole in my forehead and kill me.

"Hi, I'm—" I start to say.

"I don't care what your name is. You shouldn't be here."

"Blake, Andre is our guest, and he's—"

"Don't," Blake snaps. "Don't you dare say what I think you're about to say."

Claire sighs. "Blake. Simply because you don't want to hear it doesn't make it any less true. Andre has your brother's liver. Andre can time travel—you felt it, I felt it, your father felt it. Which means that there is someone in this world who could reveal our secret, unless they have the proper training. That's where we come in." She takes a beat. "More accurately, that's where you come in. Which is why I wanted you here on time."

"What?" Blake and I both say at the exact same time.

"Why?" Blake asks.

Claire shrugs. "It'll do you both some good. But more importantly? Your brother would have…"

"Don't." Blake is seething. "Don't use him to get what you want. You don't have the right. And *more importantly?*" he sneered, mimicking her tone. "There's no way in hell I'm teaching him how to jump."

"And who said I even believed in all this?" I add.

Blake turns to me. "Are you calling my mom a liar?"

"I didn't say that, and just one minute ago, you wanted *nothing* to do with me."

Blake takes a step forward. "I still want nothing to do with you. You're not part of this family, and you're certainly not my brother, so I'm not even sure why you're here."

"I never said I was your brother, and I'm very sorry for your loss. I'm very happy to leave, though."

The vibe I get from Blake? From this family? It's…uncomfortable, to say the least. It's like something is off, a piece is missing in a puzzle, and they're trying to compensate for it in weird ways. It's too much weirdness right now, when I have so many other things on my plate.

Before I can respond, everything changes. And Blake is gone.

And so is the view.

And the couch.

And the whole house.

Instead, I'm standing in the living room of my own house. Well, not my house. Michael's house. In 1969. *Again.* Except this time, there's jazz playing.

"Shit!"

A loud crunch makes me jump, and I quickly spin around, only to come face-to-face with Michael and his floppy blond hair. He's dressed only in boxers, with a bowl of cereal balanced precariously in the palm of his right hand, a spoon and a cigarette in his left, staring at me with a mix of elation and surprise.

"I feel," Michael says, then swallows, "like I should be concerned by how you got into my house, but we'll deal with that second. First, though…" He puts his bowl down on a stand next to a record player. "Want some cereal?"

For several seconds, I just stand there, looking at him, surveying the room, much like I did his lawn. My lawn. Whatever. I try my best to get my bearings. To deal with the millions of questions going through my head, deciding which one to ask, as if Michael could answer them.

But all that comes out is an enthusiastic and uncharacteristic…

"*Yes.*"

SEVEN

From what I can tell, Michael really likes alcohol. Especially with his cereal, a combination he claims is the *dinner of champions*.

In the ten minutes I've been here, he's already tried to make me a drink three times now. The first time, he said he didn't add enough alcohol. The second time, not enough ice. And the third time, this time, he seems to have found the right balance.

"Try this," he says, quietly padding over to me in his bare feet and handing me the drink. "You look like a dark 'n' stormy type of guy."

"Is that because I'm Black?"

Michael only smiles, leaning against the couch. The jazz has died down, leaving only the pulsing life of a bustling cul-de-sac to entertain us.

I hate jazz, something my father tries to rectify every time it comes up in conversation (or a jazz festival comes to town), but it was a nice, calming reprieve compared to the other noises. Noises that remind me that, no matter how similar it is, this isn't my home.

I stare at the brownish liquid and sigh. Why not?

It has a sharp taste to it but also a sweet aftereffect. There's ginger, definitely, and the alcohol—rum, I think—isn't as strong as I expected. The coolness of the drink feels good against my throat.

By the time I finally put the drink down, it's about a third of the way gone.

"Did I disturb you?" I ask.

Michael stares at me for a moment longer, a small hint of a grin forming on his lips. Even as he brings his cereal bowl to his lips, like I do, he doesn't stop staring. He's like a cat watching its prey, but in a more playful way.

"You're an odd one," he finally says. "But no. I just got out of the shower, and now I'm eating cereal with booze for dinner, because I'm what? An adult." A lopsided, boyish smile takes over his features. "Was playing some music to pass the time, you know? But I'd much rather spend the time with you. Get to know you, Andre from Boston, and most importantly, learn how it is that you just disappear and reappear like you did now and three days ago—"

"Wait, sorry, *what?*" I quickly interject.

"Which part didn't make sense to you?"

"The three days."

"Not the disappearing part? Because that's the part I'm curious about. Is the future really that advanced that you can just—" He snaps his fingers, demonstrating. He waits for an explanation, one I can't give him.

Michael smiles another lopsided grin that makes my heart skip a beat before he nods his head toward the wall. We both walk over to it as he points to a calendar. It's a Lord of the Rings calendar. For the month of June, it has an illustration of Pippin and Merry riding the back of the Ents.

"You disappeared here," he says, tapping the date—the fourteenth. That was the day I got home from the hospital visit. He then slides his finger across the calendar, stopping on the seventeenth. "And here's today."

"Three days," I mutter.

"Three days," he repeats.

Which doesn't fully make sense, since I know I was there... here...whatever...last night.

I feel my mind doing what it does when I'm going down a rabbit hole. It's like the walls of reality close in around me, and nothing else matters but the narrow truth in front of me. My tunnel vision, Mom always says, is what's going to make me a good doctor, because it allows me to focus on one thing and get it done. I'm not sure I agree. But right now, my mind is focused on so many things: time travel, the ramifications of it, what will happen when I get back, *if* I get back...

But the thing that sticks out the most at this moment, like a sore thumb or an iceberg painted neon, is Michael and how calm he is.

"You're not afraid." I dumbly state this, rather than ask him the question.

Michael tips his head back, and the large ice cubes in his

glass clink together and brush against his nose as he tries to get the last drop from the bottom of his drink.

"Should I be? Do I have a reason to be afraid of you, Andre?"

"Most people would be afraid of random men appearing in their house."

"You're not the first, and I *doubt* you'll be the last," he teases, putting his bowl in the sink. "And besides, you seem scared enough for the two of us. You're better dressed today, though."

I look down quickly to examine myself.

"Something about it fits you." Michael gives me another look up and down before walking to the couch and jumping over the back side of it. He heads upstairs.

Without hesitation, I follow.

When we enter a room, I realize that it's his room—and that in the 2021 floor plan, it's the upstairs living room. Mom and Dad blew the walls out in order to make the master bedroom bigger.

Michael walks over to his desk, where a record player sits, and moves the needle over the vinyl. A sharp sound fills the air, and then a soft aria ripples through the room.

"Do you know who this is?" he asks as he makes waves in the air with his fingers, which move smoothly along with the music.

"Opera?"

"I didn't ask *what*," he says, with no obvious sharpness. "I said *who*."

"A woman."

"Now you're trying to be difficult." Half a beat passes. "It's a good look on you, even if you're wrong. It's Wolfgang Amadeus Mozart. 'Der Hölle Rache kocht in meinem Herzen.'"

"Gesundheit."

Michael smiles and shakes his head, focusing on lighting a blunt between his fingers. It takes him four clicks of the lighter to finally catch it. He takes a deep drag, the end glowing a mix of blacks, oranges, and reds. As he exhales, tendrils of white smoke dance and twirl in the air, disappearing as they rise higher and higher.

"Not my thing," I say. Isobel does it, but only because of her girlfriend Stacey. Stacey always says it's not a big deal.

Yet Isobel never wants to talk about it after she's done it.

"More for me then," he replies happily, taking another long drag. Michael stretches, showing his abs, and moves to sit on the edge of the bed, crossing his legs at his ankles. He closes his eyes, rests his arms behind his head, and presses the blunt between his lips while he lazily breathes out smoke.

"As much as I love having a handsome man in the house with me, you know you're going to have to tell me how you got here, right?" he says, not opening his eyes. "Because if my parents come home and see you here, we're going to need to have our stories straight. So they don't call the pigs."

Did he just say what I think he said? Does he believe me? I fall silent thinking my word choice over.

"You're not worried about them, you know, finding alcohol and weed in here? How old are you, anyway?"

"Weed." He chuckles, opening one eye. "You sound like a white boy."

I pause, ignoring that racially loaded statement, and instead search for the right word. "Ganja?"

"Better." Michael winks, then closes his eyes again. "And I'm eighteen. You?"

"Seventeen. Going back to the topic at hand. You believe me?"

Michael shrugs and takes another drag. "Twice you've just randomly appeared. One of those times, you also randomly disappeared, and if I were a gambling man, which I am, I'd bet you'll do it again. It's not about belief anymore, it's about trusting what's in front of me. Sit."

It feels awkward to sit on the edge of the bed with my back straight, while Michael is so calm. I don't know anyone who would be so chill about someone appearing in their home. Mom and Dad would send Clyde after an intruder. Isobel would throw things, like she did during Halloween last year when we watched *The Strangers* and her dad suddenly came home.

Michael isn't like any of those people. He isn't like anyone, actually. He's slower moving, calmer. Quieter too. Like stress is something he's aware of, but he doesn't let it consume him.

I wish I were more like him.

Reluctantly, I give it a try, slowly leaning back, sinking into the bed.

"Tell you what," Michael says, turning toward me and opening his blue eyes. "Let's make a game out of it. You answer one question of mine, and I'll answer one of yours. Complete honesty. That way, if you have some silly story about how you got here, which I'm betting you do, it's an even trade. I get to hear about the future from you, and you get to hear some wild shit about the past from me. Stuff I bet isn't in your history books."

"No judgment?"

Michael shakes his head. "Besides, who am I to judge you? Like you said…" He gestures to the bowl of half-smoked weed—*ganja*—and liquor bottles. "I'm not exactly a saint."

I turn to face Michael, searching his eyes for any sort of lie. Mom says you can always tell someone's truth if you look in their eyes long enough. It's how she vets candidates before taking them on.

If someone's lying to you, stare at them, she told me on the way to mock debate finals last year. *Liars always break.*

I didn't have the heart to tell her that it sounded suspiciously like something you would do to show dominance over a dog.

But Michael doesn't waver. He holds my stare—doesn't even blink. Instead, he playfully snaps his teeth at me, laughing one of those full body laughs.

"Let's get the most awkward question out of the way first, hmm? How did you get here? By *here* I mean my house."

There's no easy way to answer that question. No way that wants to just pour out of me. I start, but it feels like my mouth is filled with hardening molasses.

What if he's asking me these questions because he doesn't

really believe me? What if he wants to lock me up or something? Can he even do that? I could just time travel away, right? But what if I can't?

But, deep down, do I really think Michael is that type of person? Even sitting here, his body so relaxed and at peace, tapping his blunt to an invisible beat, he seems...not at all worried or concerned or whatever synonym better fits the mood.

So I take a leap of faith.

"Time travel," I say in one quick breath.

It takes a moment for it to register on Michael's face, like he's not sure if I'm telling the truth.

"Oh, wait, you're serious," he says, nodding and rubbing his hands together. "Okay, I'm with you. So time travel is how you got here?"

"I think."

"You think? Like, you're not sure?"

"Before I say anything or even attempt to explain it, I want you to know that I fully understand how unreal this sounds. And no, I can't explain it.

"I have two options." I take a few moments to practice in my head what I'm going to say. "The first is that I'm dreaming, or in a medically induced coma from hitting my head, and all of the past three days is some complex hallucination that is deeply rooted in my subconscious and my desire to be someone, which has been instilled in me by my parents for as long as I can remember."

"And the other option?"

"That, somehow, I'm time traveling into the past, and I'm tied to you or this house...because this is my house in the future."

"Is that a question or a statement?"

I pause. "Both?"

The sounds of the neighborhood around us fill the air once again, plugging the space that my silence leaves. Or attempting to. Neither of us talking is a deafening thing.

"I know it sounds ridiculous," I quickly add. "Both of those options."

"Oh, they totally do. But, between you and me, number two actually makes more sense than number one."

Before I can chime in, he explains.

"Number one means that I'm just a figment of your imagination, right? If this is all a 'manifestation,' then I'm not really real. Which can't be true, since I have memories, experiences, and independent thoughts, and I can do this."

Suddenly, he leans over and presses his lips against my cheek. It feels like being burned, but in a good way, like his lips are going to leave a searing mark on my flesh that's impossible to get rid of.

Michael pulls back as if nothing happened. It's only a peck, sure. I've given Isobel more sensual kisses than that. But...the fact that he did it so casually? And that it came from a guy? It makes my cheeks burn, and my head feel dizzy.

I look over at Michael with a sideways glance, like if I move too quickly, this will all shatter. He's gone back to smoking.

"Plus, and I mean this nicely, you're definitely out of sight."

"Excuse me?"

"You dress funny. You talk funny. Hell, you *move* funny. Hence, weird. Luckily, I like weird. Especially weird, *cute* guys."

"You don't think I'm lying?" I ask, ignoring his flirting as best I can.

"We're all lying about something, Andre. And, if I may, the idea that something out there—or someone—has connected us? That out of all the gin joints in all the world you walked into mine?" He looks over, his shaggy hair now in front of his eyes. "That's unreal. And I like when things are unreal. And I prefer to think that's what this is, rather than accepting that my existence doesn't matter in the grander scheme of things."

When I was young and afraid of something, instead of comforting me with platitudes, my mother and father explained facts to me. Told me how irrational my fears were.

My family is a family of science. My father? The biological. My mother? The statistical. We don't believe in this.

But this moment, sitting here with Michael, listening to him hum under his breath to the music? It feels like magic.

EIGHT

Hanging out with Michael is as easy as breathing.

We spend hours talking and laughing. Occasionally, we argue, but it's never more than a small debate. And when we do, we pause, compare words, and make jokes at each other's expense about how different we are.

In many ways, the most important ways, I guess that makes us the same.

Sounds like the message on some half-price greeting card or something.

Until he asks me that question, sometime between four and five o'clock in the morning, that no one ever likes hearing.

"Mind if I ask you a personal question?"

I know what that means. It's like saying, *No offense, but...*

Spoiler: these questions are always, *always* offensive.

I don't look at him as he turns to face me. I keep my eyes trained ahead, memorizing the disfigured shapes formed from the warped ceiling.

"Sure."

He hesitates for a moment—for so long that the tension settles, and I think he won't ask it. A part of me prays that he won't. But Michael isn't that type of guy.

"Are you gay?"

The question comes out of left field, or at least it feels like it does. I can't remember the last time I've been asked that. I'm not saying I live some perfect life where everyone just *knows* or doesn't dare *assume*, but the question, so blunt and direct, makes me refocus my attention.

"Why does it matter?"

Michael shrugs. "Just curious."

It's a decoy answer. Something you say to relax your target before laying the real hard-hitting question or statement on them. Give them a false sense of security, and then throw them off guard.

But if I know that going in, then I have the advantage. So I bite.

"You first." I throw it back to him. It gives me a moment to think.

But Michael doesn't hesitate. "Oh, I'm gay. I mean, come on. Look at me," he teases and gives a fake muscleman pose. It causes his shirt to ride up again and his biceps, lean but well-defined muscles, to flex, and I can't help but smile.

"I look like this, and I'm going to be a world-famous musician. I can't lose."

"A world-famous musician, huh?"

He nods firmly. "You heard it here first. I'm going to

join a band, play for Wayne Shorter or Herbie Hancock or someone."

"Who?"

Michael blinks owlishly. "Seriously? You don't know who… Jazz musicians, Andre. Come on, now. You should know this."

"Because I'm Black?"

"Because you seem like a *cultured* person," he scoffs. "Do you at least know who Joan Didion is?"

I nod. "The author. Everyone knows her."

He lets out a fake deep breath. "Thank God you at least know *that* cultural icon. I want to be an author like her too. Obviously, I'm still trying to figure this whole career-for-life thing out. But I'm certain I'm going to be some kind of artist. You can put your money on that one."

I wonder, for a moment, what would happen if I told my parents I wanted to be a musician. Would they throw me out of the house? Would they even care? Music is a science and an art. Quarter notes, half notes—that's all math, and I'm good at that.

But a musician is not a doctor. Nothing else matters besides that.

"Plus, it means I get to travel. Really see the world and its people, you know? That sounds great." Out of the corner of my eye, I see him looking at me. "You never answered me."

"Yes, I'm gay," I say, as easily as he did. And, to keep with the theme of describing our futures, I add, "I want to be… I'm *going* to be a doctor." I pause. "A double doctor, actually."

He quirks his brow.

"I want to have an MD and a PhD. An MD in oncology and a PhD in biomedical research with a focus on transplant sciences, to be exact."

Michael whistles. "That's a cancer doctor, right?"

"Mm-hmm. There's something cool about taking complex problems and finding a solution that saves someone's life."

"How did you decide?"

"It's the most stable field out there. People will always get cancer," I say, which isn't a lie, but its easier than going into the whole I-had-cancer-so-it's-close-to-my-heart discussion.

Michael's face screws into a frown. "So you're doing it because it's stable? Not because you want to?"

"Can't it be both?"

"Is it both?"

A leading question, I think, but I also don't know the answer to it. Ever since I was little and told my parents that I wanted to be a doctor, they helped suggest what field I should specialize in. From a young age, the choices were limited: family medicine, oncology, or cardiovascular medicine. Cardio was quickly thrown out when it became evident that I don't have outstanding fine motor skills. And family medicine...that just seemed so boring to them.

Oncology was the right choice. The best choice. We all agreed. At least, that's how I remember it.

I shrug and give a not-quite-full answer as a reply. "Mom and Dad are both doctors, but more doctors of research. Academic ones. They have always just wanted what's best for me."

"That doesn't answer my question. Do you want to be a doctor because *you* want to be one or because your parents want you to be one?"

There it is.

"Because you seem so much more interesting than someone who does something just to please *Daddy*."

I shove him hard enough for his body to sway, but not enough to really move him.

"I'm sick. Well, I used to be sick. I still could be—who knows?"

Usually, people tense up when I say that. They back away and stumble over their words. But Michael doesn't.

In fact, he moves closer to me. Close enough that his body heat radiates against mine, warming my skin. The faint smell of cigarette smoke is stronger than it was a few moments ago but not overpowering.

"Like, *sick* sick?"

I shake my head. "You can't catch it. Don't worry."

"I wasn't."

"I have—*had* cancer a while back."

Michael sits up on his elbows, eyes wide. It's not the usual reaction I get from people when I tell them that, but it's similar. Surprise. Pity. Fear. All rolled into one neat package.

"Seriously? You okay?"

I nod again. "Cancer of the liver." I pull up my shirt, showing him the scar. I wince as his fingers move gently over it, tracing the rivers and valleys from the sutures.

"Sorry."

"It doesn't hurt."

"Oh, so you're just ticklish. Noted."

"I'm just not used to someone doing that. Anyway, it's what gave me this ability to travel."

He gives me a puzzled look.

"Long story. Circles back to what I said before—about, you know, time travel."

"We've got time." He grins in a boyish way that shows off dimples I've never noticed before.

In response, I hit him with my foot. "I got this cancer thanks to a hepatocellular carcinoma; you don't need to remember that."

"Thank God."

"I want to find a cure for it. That's why I want to become a doctor. I'll go to an Ivy for undergrad, then Harvard for medical school and my doctorate. New York for my postdoc. And we'll see what happens there."

"No breaks?" Michael asks, obviously surprised.

"I don't have time for that."

Michael sits up. "Don't stop now. You have your whole life planned out. Why stop ten years from now? Why not keep going? How about twenty years from now? Or thirty?"

My chest tightens, only for a moment, in a twinge of annoyance that I know will spread like thick, hot lava if I don't tame it.

"What would you prefer I do?" I ask. "Flap around in the wind like you? See what happens?"

"There's a space between trying to control everything, which yields no control, and just leaving it up to luck. You're young, Andre! You're..."

"Don't," I warn. And before he can ask, I add, "Don't tell me that I'm young and that I have my whole life ahead of me. Don't act like my parent."

"That wasn't at all what I was going to say."

"Sure." I wave my hand in a wide arc, in a "*the floor is yours*" sort of way.

"What I was *going* to say was, your life is your own. You don't owe anyone anything. Not your parents. Not society. You can take this opportunity to live life to the fullest. So I'm here to ask you: Are you going to medical school because *you* want to or because your *parents* want you to?"

The molten hot lava inside bursts into pure white rage. How dare this guy judge me? What right does he have? How long has he known me? A few hours?

"What makes you think this isn't what I want?"

"Maybe it is. But that's not the vibe I get."

Deep down, somewhere dark and damp, with locks upon locks, I know that being judged isn't what made my hackles rise. It's the small pilot light that Michael has stoked. The small flame he's given life to that had been forced into silence months ago and had stayed silent. That small voice that asked, *What about photography or writing or music? What about trying something new? That's what college is for, right?*

It was the voice of rebellion that I killed long ago.

The perfect quippy arrowhead of a comeback is right on the tip of my tongue. But before I can fire it, a rush of air suddenly swirls around me. Colors mix, and the ground rises up faster than it should, like I'm crashing in reverse. It happens so fast this time that I'm barely able to prepare myself for it. In a heartbeat, I'm standing back in the McIntyres' home.

No, not standing—sitting in the middle of the living room.

Claire doesn't even seem phased when she looks up from the mantel where she's leaning.

"Welcome back," she says, checking her watch. She walks over and grabs my hand, helping me stand before dusting me off, much like a mother would. "You were gone roughly three minutes, by the way. I imagine your friend Isobel is going to be coming in very soon, so we don't have much time. You should start wearing a watch—it's going to be your most valuable tool as a traveler. How was the trip?"

I stand there dumbstruck. It takes me a few seconds to get my bearings. To shake off the jet lag of traveling through time and space. There's a dull, almost mistakable throb in the pit of my stomach, but I think that's just nerves. Besides, I have bigger things to worry about.

"Wait, wait, three minutes? How..."

"How can that be?" Claire finishes for me. "Rule of thumb. One hour whenever you travel is one minute in your current time period. It's a simple rule to remember. Not one of the three cardinal rules, but..."

She keeps talking, but her words fade out and sound fuzzy as my mind seems to disassociate from my body.

My name is Andre Cobb. I'm seventeen years old, born and raised in Boston, Massachusetts. I'm a cancer survivor and a student at St. Clements Academy. I'm the son of Jennifer Cobb and Daniel Cobb, and the most unique thing about me?

"I'm a time traveler."

Claire grins brightly. Her hands find their way to my shoulders, and she squeezes. "That you are."

Holy fucking shit.

NINE

Mom and Dad were already pissed when Isobel and I came home late. Not as pissed as Isobel was when I wouldn't share any information with her about what had happened inside the McIntyres' house, but close.

"Where were you?"

"Out with Isobel."

"Where did you go?"

"The McIntyres'."

They pause, confused.

"They're the family who gave me my liver," I say, clarifying.

Mom's eyes grow wide, and Dad spits up the drink he's sipping.

"That's not…" Dad starts but pauses.

"Protocol," Mom says. "That's not protocol."

"They reached out."

"How did they find your number?"

"I don't know."

"What did you say?"

I shrug. "They just wanted to check in, see how I was doing. I thought I owed it to them, considering." I point to my liver. "You know."

Mom's face goes on a journey of expressions: frustration, then confusion, then indecision, before finally resting on understanding.

"I told them thank you," I say. "They're nice people, Mom."

"I'm sure they are," she says in a way that's not fully condescending, but not fully convincing either. She's still processing everything that's happened. We're not so different in that regard.

"Can I go upstairs? I'm feeling a bit tired."

"Sure, champ," Dad says. I'm sure he and Mom want to talk about me visiting the McIntyres'. Surviving cancer gives me some leeway, but the rope isn't endless.

I take the steps two at a time, close my door behind me, and take a deep breath for what feels like the first time since I got in the car with Isobel. The world just needs to slow down for a moment.

I change into my pajamas for the night and flop into bed.

Twenty minutes after dozing off, I feel my phone vibrate. A text appears from Claire.

617-555-1431. Blake's phone number.

When you're ready.

"When I'm ready," I repeat. When is anyone ready to learn how to time travel? How do you wrap your head around that? And I'm pretty sure Blake is *not* keen on teaching me.

That doesn't matter. Right now, the only thing I need to focus on is getting sleep, going back to my normal routine, and figuring out how I'm going to be myself, when I haven't felt like myself in almost a year—most of all now.

Problems for future Andre.

———————
———————

Headmistress Welchbacher has silvery hair that she pulls back into a bun and sharp features that make her bone structure look modelesque, which I can't help but notice as she examines my file for a good three minutes with her bright blue eyes. The only sound is the metronome on her desk ticking back and forth.

There are three certainties in the world: death, taxes, and that Headmistress Welchbacher and I greatly dislike each other.

I wouldn't go so far as to say she's racist—that's a bold claim. But she's never liked me. Maybe because I started out as a scholarship kid here. Or maybe because my mom beat out her best friend for PTA president. Who knows, really. There are lots of possible explanations for why she turns her nose up at me, takes longer to answer my family's emails, and does half a dozen other small things that no one else notices.

But the way she reads my file, slower than need be, and doesn't even say hello or ask how I'm feeling when I enter always sets me off.

"So, you're feeling better?" she finally asks, after five minutes of me sitting there, listening to the obnoxious sound of the metronome on top of her desk. I wonder how many music students here have PTSD from that constant sound.

"Yes, Headmistress Welchbacher, thanks for asking." I know she only did it as a formality, but maybe thanking her will make her feel guilty.

"Good, good. Now…" She pulls out a second file—thicker, but just as organized as everything else in this room. It's almost more sterile than a hospital. "About your graduation…"

This is exactly why I came here and what I've been waiting for. I'm sure she has more than a dozen reasons why I should stay back. I'm sure they are all well within the school's guidelines, and I'm sure she's been waiting with great anticipation for the past month to tell me those reasons.

But I have something she doesn't. Determination.

"Ms. Harper said I could take summer school courses to complete the three I missed last semester," I remind her, pulling out a crumpled printout of the email from my canvas messenger bag. Headmistress Welchbacher takes it, grabbing it by two fingers only, and looks at it with disgust.

"She's not wrong, but you understand…"

"I'll lose my salutatorian status, yes, I know."

Headmistress Welchbacher pauses, glancing up at me. She doesn't like being interrupted. That's 60 percent of why I did it. The other 40 percent is that I don't like being around her for any longer than I have to be.

I don't like being held back because of something out of my control.

"That's correct. You'll need to take calculus, a history class, and a creative elective."

"A community college nearby has all those classes."

"Will you be able to register in time? There are only two months left of summer. I'm worried."

No you're not. You're hoping that I can't, I think. But Mom and I already talked about this possibility when a transplant was first discussed. Silently, I pull out another piece of paper.

"I've already registered for Calc One, History of the Modern World, and a creative writing class. All of these start online next week, and they fulfill the Northeastern collegiate requirements for learning that St. Clements abides by."

Headmistress Welchbacher's jaw tightens as she examines the documents, searching for any reason to say that the classes won't work. But I got up early today when I couldn't sleep and spent all morning before this meeting double- and triple-checking them. These classes are perfect. And considering that St. Clements has an agreement with the community college that allows juniors and seniors to take part-time classes there, this should be easy.

"I suppose these will work," she concedes.

"Excellent."

I put the document back in my bag, swinging it over my shoulder.

"Andre," she says when I reach the door. "Our standards here at St. Clements are high. Higher than a public school. You'll need to earn a minimum of an eighty-eight in each of your classes for them to count."

"They only do letter grades there."

"A B plus then."

"And if they don't do pluses and minuses?"

"An A."

Of course.

I nod to her curtly before slipping out and letting the heavy oak door shut loudly behind me. There aren't many students here, only those attending the summer programs for kindergarten through third grade, as well as a few students interning from other schools, hoping to bolster their applications to St. Clements or to college.

I make my way down the hallway, turn left, and weave through the school, taking a shortcut to the back parking lot, where the Camry sits. I've walked these halls thousands of times since coming here in ninth grade. Things were good. Like, really good.

And then? Shit hit the fan.

I stop at the wooden bench that faces the south lawn, running my fingers over the polished wood. There are three indentations on the arm, small ones, but they are the only imperfections on the bench. And they're from me.

I remember the pain that shot through my body like a bolt of electricity. I remember gripping the wood so hard that my nails cracked, leaving those marks. I remember collapsing and some senior finding me. And then I remember waking up in the hospital.

The pain and the humiliation isn't what I remember most.

What I remember most is feeling like I didn't have control over my life.

But now I do. And now I have an ability that I never knew was possible. What limits are there to time travel? Can I see problems around the world and fix them? Can I fix my own timeline? Right my past mistakes?

What can I do, and what can't I do?

That's a question that only one person can help me answer.

"Damn it." I sigh, pulling out my phone. I find the text from Claire, tap it, and call Blake. The phone rings twice.

"Blake?"

He hesitates. "Yeah?"

"It's Andre. Andre Cobb." I'm not sure how he's going to respond, so I wait. After a moment, I say, "From last night?"

"I remember you. What's up? How did you get this number?"

"Your mom, of course."

He sighs. "Of course."

"Yeah, seems like she's…"

"A lot?" he offers. "You have no idea. Or do you? Not sure how the whole transference of someone else's organ works when it comes to memories."

I want to tell him that's stupid, but then I remember that my time-travel abilities are something I got from an organ, so I settle on saying, "Fair." Then I continue, knowing that if I stop, I'll lose steam and hang up. "I don't know if you're busy, but… I wanted to see if we could talk."

"Is this about what my mom proposed last night?"

"Mm-hmm."

"I have a few hours before practice. Come on over. I'll make smoothies. You like berry ones, right? With Greek yogurt and just the right amount of mango?"

The description makes my mouth water, for good reason. "How did you…"

"Three years ago, when your mom was diagnosed as prediabetic, she started to change her diet. You and your dad joined in, a whole family endeavor, to be healthier for her. She got her numbers to a better place in a few months, and you learned how to cook. One of your favorite things to make was a berry smoothie, with Greek yogurt and just the right amount of mango.

"Time travel isn't just about going to the past or seeing amazing historical moments. It's about reliving the small moments too. Like the first time you made a smoothie and walked to the store by yourself to get the ingredients, so you could make it for her when she came home from work. A person who cares that much about such a small thing is someone…" He sighs, pausing for a moment. The blender stops. "Just come over. Don't make me say please."

"What are you, some sort of vampire who is weakened by displaying any sort of manners?"

He laughs on the phone, but it's not an actual laugh. It's hollow and forced, but I applaud the effort.

It's only ten o'clock in the morning, but already the sun is starting to warm not only the asphalt but also my own dark skin. Beads of sweat form and ripples of clear heat rise from the parking lot. The memory is something so small, so insignificant. But now, hearing Blake talk about it? It brings back every sense. The smell of the fresh rain that afternoon. The weight of the bag I carried a mile and a half home. The tourists in the store with me and their bright "We're from Kansas, Say Hi!" shirts.

"You're a time traveler and a stalker, a bad combo if you ask me, Blake McIntyre from Boston."

"Wrong and wrong on both counts. But how about you come over, and I'll tell you the truth, the whole truth. And why did you just say my name like that?"

"No reason." That's a lie, but I quickly answer his question. "On my way."

TEN

When I arrive at the McIntyres' home, Blake is shirtless, wearing a pair of workout sweats that he obviously cut into shorts himself.

He's standing at the front door, leaning against it, chewing on a half-consumed green apple. He doesn't move to greet me, except for giving a short wave when I park the car.

"Not even a hello?" I ask.

He only shrugs.

Part of me wonders if I should follow him. Maybe I should play this like a game of chicken. Make him say *something* to me, instead of just *assuming* that I'm going to trot after him. It's a power move, after all, and playing into it is like giving unlimited oxygen to a house fire.

But then again, he has all the knowledge, which gives him the power, and there's nothing I can do except play his game.

For now.

Before I can step over the threshold, he speaks without bothering to turn around.

"Take your shoes off," he shouts.

I toss them into the corner before following his voice into the kitchen. There he is, leaning against the counter, swiping idly through his phone, his right bicep slightly flexed. He doesn't look up but gestures toward two glasses on the counter. Sure enough, they are filled with the same purple-colored smoothie that I remember making dozens of times.

"Let me know if I made it right. Not sure I got the percentages down. Do you use whole milk or skim milk?"

"Whole. But I've switched to oat milk recently."

"Of course you have," he mutters.

I walk around the other side of the counter, taking the drink and sipping it slowly. From the thickness, I can tell that there's a little too much yogurt, and from the tartness, I can tell that it's the plain kind.

"So you can do it too?" I ask.

Blake looks up from his phone, turning it screen-side down. For the first time, I notice that he has the most beautiful green eyes I've ever seen. The type that look like some sort of biosphere lives and thrives inside of them.

"Yes and no."

"I feel like 'can you time travel' isn't the type of question that can yield a 'maybe.'"

"Har har," he says. "I can't. Mom did it. She likes…learning about people. It's the scientist in her."

"What's her field?"

Blake shrugs. "She's a self-proclaimed scientist. Mom's

actually a lawyer. The fancy type that helps foundations keep out of legal trouble. But I think, deep down, all time travelers think they are scientists. I mean, if you can observe and make logical deductions about anything in the world, in any time period, isn't that what a scientist is?"

"Not really," I say bluntly.

Blake chuckles mid-sip and hisses. "Smoothie went up my nose." He turns and grabs a napkin, blowing his nose loudly.

"So she…"

"Stalked you through time? Yes." He empties his glass and puts it in the dishwasher, closing it with his foot. "Creepy, right?"

"Extremely."

"Welcome to my life."

Blake gets a new glass from the top shelf and pours himself the remainder of the smoothie from the blender. I have half a mind to ask him why he got a new glass, but I know the answer: rich white wastefulness. He's probably never been told not to run the dishwasher with only half a load. Or to make sure he has all the clothes he needs for the week in the laundry because there won't be another chance to do it this weekend. That's what happens when you're rich.

"I was an ass when you came over to visit," he says.

"You were justified. I mean, this is a lot."

He shrugs. Again. "Sure, but it's a lot for you, too, I imagine. Learning that you can time travel. Meeting the family of the person who gave you his liver. It's a lot to take in, and I should have…considered that before lashing out."

Blake reaches back with his right hand, rubbing the back of his head. My breath hitches. It's a beautiful sight, the way his abs flex and his skin stretches, how his bicep shows. It's almost model-worthy, the type of pose and body that you think is unobtainable, just a figment of reality crafted by the beauty industry. But Blake actually has it. The strong pecs. The V in his hips.

Riverdale should just cast him right now.

"Ask anything you want," he offers. "Any question that you think you need to know to help you process this. I know it's a lot. Trust me, I grew up in a family of time travelers and it's *still* sometimes too much for me."

"To clarify, you're offering me a free pass."

"Mm-hmm."

"On anything?"

"Well, if you asked me if I wear boxers or briefs, that's probably not the best use of your question, but I'd answer anyway."

"Trust me, that's not a question I'm going to be asking you."

But there are a lot of others: the rules of time travel, why he isn't able to do it, what the limitations are, the consequences. All logical questions that a scientist would ask. All questions that my parents would ask.

And something about that makes me feel sick.

Ever since I can remember, I've been compared to them. I've been told that I have my father's knack for quick thinking. My mother's skill in logical deduction. Two years ago, one of Dad's colleagues said that I was the perfect mix of both of them.

And it never struck me how screwed up it is to say that to someone.

I like being like my parents. But I don't want to be a perfect copy of them. I want to be my own person. That's what everyone wants, right? Call it a teenage cliché or the need to rebel, but it's true.

"Can I get...three questions?"

Blake's brow furrows for a moment. It's like watching something click in his head in real time. "You asked for three instead of two because you knew I'd say that question right there was one question, didn't you?"

"You're smarter than you look," I fire back.

"Some of us have beauty *and* brains. It's possible, you know." He gestures. "Go ahead."

So I do something that my parents would never do: I ask a completely off-the-wall question.

"Is your dad's hair naturally brown, or does he dye it?"

Blake stops mid-sip, slowly putting his glass down. He doesn't even swallow the mouthful of liquid for a moment, not until his mind seemingly remembers that he's holding it in his mouth. He gives an exaggerated gulp, never looking away from me.

"Let me get this straight. I just confirmed a family secret that only about a dozen people in the world know, and you're concerned about my father's hair color?"

I nod. "It's for science."

"You know time travel is science, too, right?"

"Science fiction, maybe."

"Science fiction is something that's not real."

"I'm still not completely convinced that I'm not losing my mind—or that I'm not in a coma and this is just some fabrication that my brain has made up to help me deal with some horrific trauma."

"Are you always like this?"

"All the time."

"So, Mr. I'm-Stuck-in-Some-Dantesque-Coma, what do you think all this is?" He gestures toward the smoothies.

"A lucky guess?"

"You're stubborn as hell."

"You'll grow to love it."

A slow grin spreads over Blake's face as he crosses his strong, well-defined arms over his broad, bare chest. "Naturally that color."

"So, you're the lucky one," I reason. "There was a fifty-fifty chance that you'd get the gene for red hair. Well, you might still have it, actually. But a fifty-fifty chance that it would manifest. Your brother got it. You didn't. It's basic science, really."

"That's not basic at all," he replies.

"If you pay attention in science class—genotypes and phenotypes—it is."

Personally, I think the tidbit about red hair is interesting. It's a mutation, after all. A dying out one at that. But Blake's sullen face proves that he doesn't think the same. His muscles tighten, and he looks sharper, more angular and threatening than he did before, when his edges were rounder. Quickly, he stands, taking his glass and rinsing it out.

"That's another thing David got that I didn't," he mutters.

The tension in the room instantly becomes so thick that it's hard to breathe, and to combat it, I check my phone. Two texts from Isobel and one from my mom asking how the meeting went. Before I can finish my informative three-sentence reply, Blake says, "Here's the deal. I didn't call you back for smoothies or to talk about genealogy."

"Technically, I called you, but…point taken."

Blake rolls his eyes. "My mom is, frankly, obsessed with time travel. She's been looking for other people like us, our family, for…I think her whole life. There aren't many. It's a dying genetic trait."

"Like red hair."

"Get over the red hair, but yes."

"All right, next question then."

"There's *more*?"

"How much do you know?"

Blake arches his right brow. "About time travel?"

"That, yes, but also about…me and my ability to do it."

"About as much as you do," he says honestly. "This isn't normal. I'm not sure how long it'll last. I don't think anyone is. You're, in some ways, a new breed of time traveler—don't let that go to your head."

"Already has."

"I could've sworn your head looked bigger. But I do know

that you need to learn how to control it. Because what you don't want happening is you time traveling to the wrong time period and dying or getting stuck or jumping at the worst possible time or… Well, a lot of things can go wrong."

"Wait, sorry, pause. That can happen?"

"Amy Grant. My mom's great-grandaunt. Traveled back to the fifteenth century and landed in a river. Couldn't swim. Drowned. Ian McIntyre. My father's grandfather. Traveled back to the Civil War. Stood in the path of a musket and jumped back just in time to die on the living room floor. Oliver…"

I hold up my hand. "I get it."

"You sure? Because I have about a dozen more."

"What changed? Three days ago, you wanted nothing to do with me."

"A lot can change in three days."

"Your mother forced you, didn't she?"

"Correct." He juts his head toward the living room. He walks. I follow.

When I enter the room, Blake's already sitting on the couch, his right leg under his left.

"I have a proposition for you."

Well, that doesn't sound good. But what other choice do I have? Right now, Blake is my only hope if I want to understand any of this.

"Let me guess, you'll tell me about time travel—"

"And, in exchange, you'll do something for me in the future," Blake interrupts.

And there it is.

I cross my arms and shake my head. "A blank check IOU? Those never end well for the recipients."

"You know what doesn't end well? My mother as your teacher. She's a tyrant, Andre."

"That's just what men call a woman who has the confidence to demand the best results from the people around her," I say, quoting word for word what Isobel once said to a guy in a movie theater who called her a bitch for outsmarting him in trivia.

"Oh my God," Blake groans, flopping back on the couch. He rests his feet against the arm of it, covering his eyes with his forearm. Lying there, he lets out a loud breath, which for a moment makes his abs look even more defined than they already are.

"Wouldn't you rather work with me than my mother? Someone your own age? Someone dashing and charming and with a six-pack?"

"Are you flexing your abs right now?"

"Are you looking?"

I shake my head. I totally was.

He grins and shrugs. "I'm not going to ask you to crash the stock market or get me, like, Martin Luther King Jr.'s tie or anything like that. It's going to be something small. I promise."

"But you don't know what it is yet?"

He shakes his head and sits up. "Probably something borderline illegal. Enough to piss off my parents but not, you know, actually screw up time. Don't worry, we'll cross that bridge when we get there." He extends his hand. "So do we have ourselves a deal, Andre?"

"I'm not going to call you master or anything like that." I shake his hand firmly—that's what confident people do. "For now."

"Ah, an alliance of convenience. I'm going to like you."

In response, I roll my eyes. "So when do we start?"

He doesn't miss a beat. "Are you free now?"

"I can make time."

"See, you're already doing well. Time-travel humor. That's a key part of being one of us."

He stands up and walks by me, leaving the living room, then turning down the hall, expecting me to follow. Part of me wants to be stubborn and not follow him. To remind him that he should *ask* people before just assuming.

But curiosity gets the better of me. There's a whole world in front of me, a world I didn't know was possible, and Blake is my ticket to knowing more about time travel.

And I want to know everything.

PART TWO

ELEVEN

"There are three main rules that every time traveler needs to follow before they jump."

Blake and I are in the study as he lectures me about the dos and don'ts of time travel. He's walking around at a hurried, anxious pace that makes me feel sick, and he's pulling random books off the shelves, checking them, and deciding whether to put them in a stack in front of me or put them back on the shelf.

"One—you can't go forward, only backward."

"And why can we only go backward?"

"It's more of a societal rule than an actual physical one," he says, clarifying. "We're not supposed to take knowledge from the future and bring it back. Like, you can't go forward, discover how to make…say, a worthy competitor to the iPhone because one exists in twenty years, and then bring it back and make it yourself. It's frowned upon."

"So, it's not really a rule?"

"No, it's a rule." He slams a large book shut, and dust flies everywhere. "It's the most important rule."

"Then why are there two other rules?"

"Because…" He groans and puts the book down. "You're annoying; you know that?"

"It's a gift, really."

He sits down at the desk across from me, and pulls on a shirt, a jersey with a hawk on it: the Hutcherson Hawks. It fits him well, that elite private school whose tuition is $3,000 more than mine per semester. I don't have much room to complain. It doesn't matter what private school you go to in Boston; most of them are good. No…great. That's what Isobel said, at least.

We're all going somewhere, she reminded me one day. *Whether you go to Hutcherson or St. Clements, we're privileged enough to afford these schools. There's no reason to fight over which is better.*

Easy for her to say, since she got into both of them.

"Hey!"

A sharp snap in my face jolts me out of my thoughts. I twitch and glare at Blake. "Not cool. Don't snap in my face."

"Don't zone out, then. I'm not taking time out of my day to watch you go…wherever it is you go. I have things to do, you know? I'm doing this—"

"—out of the goodness of your heart?"

"There can be more than one reason to do something, Dre."

"Andre," I correct him. "My friends call me Dre. We're not friends. You're my teacher, and that's a very different relationship."

Blake's jaw tightens. Maybe that was a bit too harsh, but I'm not going to take it back now. Blake helping me doesn't

100

mean that I have to be nice to him. It means that I have to respect his teachings and treat this seriously.

"Fine. Rule two...only one jump at a time. You can't go to one place and then jump to another place. You have to return home."

"Like a yo-yo."

Blake rolls his eyes. "Yes, Andre. Like a human yo-yo."

"Are you going to let me ask why we have to go from point A to point B and back, or am I going to be shot down for that too?"

"Are you just going to ask annoying questions over and over again?"

"Probably."

Blake sighs, pinching his nose. He leans against the desk, which wheezes under his weight. His bicep flexes instinctively, and I do my best not to stare. It's a normal human reaction, right? Finding beauty and recognizing it in front of you? Blake's good-looking, objectively speaking.

"About your question... I'm not exactly sure."

A fake gasp leaves my mouth. "What? *The* Blake McIntyre doesn't know the answer to something?"

"God," he growls, pushing off the desk. "Bite me, Andre. I'm not a science nerd like you and my mom and..."

He falls silent, and his eyes darken. His body stiffens for a moment, like how people tighten right before a nurse gives them a shot or someone hits them.

Then, as quickly as he disappeared, he returns, snapping back into his body like... Well, just like a yo-yo.

"Where did you go?"

"Hmm?"

"Right then, you stopped in the middle of a sentence. Like you were thinking about something."

He pushes his lips into a thin line. "It was nothing."

"I'd reckon it was obviously something."

"I said it was nothing!"

His voice hits like a wave of ice-cold water. Now it's my turn to tense up. Blake runs his fingers through his hair, sighing so hard that his nostrils flare. For two minutes, he makes himself busy, moving books, organizing papers, changing objects around, and making sure of his tactile sense.

"What you're doing? All that touching? It helps you stay grounded, right? I do it, too, except for me, it's pacing."

At first, he doesn't respond; he only hesitates, as if he's been discovered. Then, slowly, he turns to me, but he doesn't move any closer. He keeps the distance—because, I can only guess, the distance makes him feel safe—and crosses one leg over the other.

"I was going to say I'm not a scientist like you, my mom, or my brother."

Ah. Of course. The dead brother. Great job poking the sore spot, Andre.

"David, right?"

"Dave. Only Mom and Dad called him David. He hated it."

"Dave," I repeat slowly. I make a mental note to remember that. "Were you two close?"

102

Before I can finish, Blake's already pulling out his wallet. He tosses it to me, and the first thing I see, besides his ID, is a photo of him and his brother.

"We weren't as close as some people are with their siblings," he admits. "But we were there for each other when it counted. He was family."

"That doesn't mean that you liked each other," I say gently. "Not everyone likes their family. You don't have to like them. Only love them."

This time, Blake opens his mouth to speak, but no sound comes out. I don't blame him. It's a hard question, deciding whether you like or love a family member. Everyone wants to think that they like their family, but that's not always the case. That's a luxury. And once you realize that? Things become...tricky.

I'm lucky enough to like and love my parents. Maybe that expression "Money can't buy happiness" really is true.

"But—more importantly, what's rule number three?" I ask. Might as well try to bring back his focus. "You said there are three rules; you only gave me two."

Blake hesitates, but I can see him slowly restarting. "Yeah, right. The rules," he mutters. "Rule number three, and this is kind of an all-encompassing rule: don't try to change anything that happens in the past. Don't take anything, don't change anything. You should go and come back and leave no evidence of your existence.

"Which reminds me..." Blake moves close, completely invading my personal space, and starts patting me down.

"Hey!" I try to swat him away, but he bats my hands, like someone brushing off a child who keeps fidgeting.

"You didn't take anything with you, did you? From before? When you jumped?"

I shake my head. "No, I didn't. Get *off of me*!" I shove him, firmly enough that his sturdy body separates from me. "That would create some sort of paradox, right?"

"That only happens if you interact with yourself in the past, idiot."

"Don't call me an idiot," I warn.

"Don't say dumb things. And besides, that only happens if you touch yourself or your past self sees you. Not the other way around. And I highly doubt you saw yourself in... Where did you go, anyway?"

"Same place as before."

"Which is?"

"Boston. Nineteen sixty-nine. My house, actually."

"The one you live in now?"

"Gee, what brought you to that conclusion?"

"Don't be a smart aleck."

"Don't say dumb things."

Blake grins at me, and I smile back. The tit for tat is a different dance than the one with Isobel. Usually, she'll get angry and defensive if I say something that offends her, even if she started it. And most of our arguments end with me conceding, because that's just better for our relationship. But with Blake, the tango is fun.

"There's a guy there, in my house back then. He lives there in sixty-nine. Both times I traveled, I went to him. The first time, I appeared on the lawn, and he was there five seconds later. The next time, I was inside of the house. It's like, I dunno…"

"You're either tethered to him or to the house."

He doesn't give me time to ask him what the hell he means before he starts to explain.

"Time travel is all about focus. If you don't know how to control it, you'll jump by accident. I'm guessing that when you jump, it's because some part of you, consciously or subconsciously, doesn't want to be where you are. Fight-or-flight reactions, anger, longing—all of these things trigger the automatic response to be somewhere else. Often the first jump is tied to some thought or memory.

"But sometimes, for whatever reason, people get bound to other people through time and space. No one knows why it happens; typically, there's some genetic or spiritual or emotional connection. So it could just be the house. Or it could be that you and…"

"Michael."

"This Michael guy and you are connected. It might be because you live in the same house. Or it could have something to do with the person you're going to become or with something he will do that directly affects you.

"If it's him you're tethered to, then whenever you think of him or have an emotional response to something, you can travel to him. It's like an express highway in time that leads to him. At any time in his existence. All you need to do is think about him, and"—Blake snaps—"you're there."

I try to remember anything about Michael that jumps out to me. He's a bit broken but charming. He seems unmoored but smart and brave. He seems like the type of guy I could see doing great things in his life, if he works at it—but connected? Us?

"It feels like you jumped to that conclusion without enough evidence."

"Spoken like a scientist." Blake grins. "Try it. The next time you want to jump somewhere intentionally, focus on him, and see what happens. That'll prove what you're tethered to.

"A tether is also your default. It's like…your lifeline. If you jump in a panic, and you need someplace safe to be, that's your home base. It's a rare thing, being bound to someone, but it can happen."

"How rare?"

Blake shrugs. "The only person I know who was also tethered was Dave." He hesitates again but recovers quickly. "But he was tethered to someone inside of our family."

"Maybe I'm able to tether because he did, and I have his organ?"

Blake shrugs. "Maybe. Time travelers are obsessed with tethers, though. You're unique for being able to do it."

Questions brew inside of me. Blake knows a lot about time travel but has never managed a jump himself. It's like he's on the edge of the conversation, absorbing it all, but never inserting himself inside of it. Like how a moon orbits a planet.

"You wouldn't happen to have any genetic connection to whomever you're jumping to, would you? This Michael guy?"

I shake my head.

"You sure?"

"Considering he's as white as snow, yeah, I'm sure."

"That technically doesn't—"

I arch a brow. "Are you about to school me on race theory right now?"

"Point taken." A beat passes before Blake speaks again. "Maybe it's something to do with your house?"

"It's just a house," I counter.

"You'd be surprised what type of energy some locations can hold. Ley lines are real, but that's a conversation for another day."

Blake walks around the desk and moves to stand close to me—like, really close.

"Stand up, will you?" he asks.

Without hesitation, like his voice is some sort of lure, I do. He smiles that boyish grin that I'm sure makes the girls at Hutcherson weak in the knees.

"You'll forgive me for this."

"What are you talking about?"

"You know how people say, 'Don't think about elephants,' and then that's all you can think about?"

I nod slowly, hesitantly.

"Don't think about Michael."

"What are y—"

Before I can finish my sentence, he grabs my shoulder and kicks my right leg out from under me. As I lose my balance, he turns my body, spinning me around so that I'm poised to fall directly on the glass coffee table.

But I never hit glass.

It's the floor—a wooden floor inside some industrial building that's neither an apartment nor a workspace.

This time, I don't lie there. I don't stare up at the sky, wondering why it's black when just seconds before it was blue and I was inside.

I know what happened.

I know where I am.

And I know, if I just look around…if I focus…

"Dre?"

I turn toward the direction of the voice and see Michael standing in the doorway, keys in hand, his mouth slightly open in surprise.

I'm sure I'm looking at him the same way he's looking at me, but I force a smile on my face and ask, "You free?"

TWELVE

"I'm sorry, how long has it been?"

The words that leave Michael's mouth don't make sense. Seven months? How can that be? Did I really get lobbed into the space-time continuum and spit out that far off course?

"Give or take a few days, yeah," he says, correcting himself as he shoves papers into his messenger bag. I catch a glimpse of them before they disappear—sheet music. "Close to seven months."

I look around, feeling for the first time since arriving the chill in the air. This building isn't his home. It's like one of those loft apartments that some people lust after. But this is too cluttered to be an apartment. Too many tables, filing cabinets...

"Do you work here?"

He nods while he finishes packing. "For now, yeah. A lot has changed since you've been gone, Dre."

"Is that a good thing or a bad thing?"

He shrugs, and a smile takes over his lips. It's one of those sad smiles, the ones that are heavy with emotion, an emotion that he doesn't want to share with me yet. "Depends on how you think about it, I guess. Come on. Are you hungry? I'm guessing that jumping through time leaves you starving."

I'm not hungry, but if eating means spending time with him…

"Yeah, I could eat."

A grin of childlike joy spreads over his face. "Then I know the perfect place."

I follow Michael out of the building and down two flights of stairs. I can hear muffled but loud sounds through the walls. It sounds like people yelling, but it's too loud for that. Too many noises—explosions, yelling, arguments. It almost seems like…

"Are we above a movie theater?"

"Yep." He pushes the door open and holds it for me. The Boston chill hits me like a close yet overly aggressive friend, but I welcome it with open arms. It's a familiar feeling, and right now, I appreciate something familiar.

"I work for a newspaper. Well, it's not a newspaper yet, it's just a collection of people like me who want to have our voices heard, reporting on things that are important to people like us. It keeps me busy, which is good, since…"

"Since what?" I ask as his voice trails off.

"Never mind, let's get going."

It's only been seven months, and the changes are subtle, but Michael has changed. He's thinned out just a bit, and his bone structure is more pronounced. He's no longer wearing jeans and a T-shirt but a khaki trench coat, a gray turtleneck, and gray pants.

He looks older, not just physically.

"What do you mean 'people like me'?" I ask. The first place my mind goes? White people, which sends a chill down my spine. A newspaper for white people doesn't sound like anything anyone should be part of. But also, Michael doesn't seem like the type of person who would participate in anything like that.

But then again, a lot can change in seven months.

"Gay people," he says without hesitation and turns the corner. "It's a paper for gay people. Somewhere we can get our news. For us, by us."

"FUBU," I say, then pause. "Sorry, you don't know what that is yet."

Michael looks puzzled, but then he chuckles. "How long until I do?"

"What year is it? Nineteen seventy?"

He nods.

"Then, about twenty-two years."

"I'll make sure to remember that. Maybe I'll look you up in ninety-two."

"I won't be born yet, but sure, wait about twelve years, and then you can."

That makes me wonder, what is the age difference between Michael and me? A quick calculation answers my question for me. If Michael is nineteen now, in 1970, that means he was born in 1951. In 2021, right now, he's seventy. Assuming that he's still alive, he's only fifteen years older than my father and eighteen years older than my mother.

Which means... I suddenly stop in my tracks. Michael turns to look at me, brow raised.

"My mom and dad," I mutter, looking at him but past him. "They are both alive right now. My dad is...four years old. My mom... Wait, what month is it?"

"January," he says. "You missed a great New Year's Eve party."

"Yeah, my mom just turned one."

Michael reaches out and squeezes my shoulders, his hands warm and grounding. It's like by rubbing them up and down, slowly, soothingly, he helps calm me.

"Do you want to go find them?" he asks, breaking the silence and pulling me out of the depths of an existential crisis that threatens to engulf me.

I snap my eyes up. "Wait, what?"

He shrugs. "I mean, do you want to?"

I open my mouth twice and close it twice. Is that even possible? Can we? Blake told me not to meet my past self, but there has to be some rule against talking to my parents before I'm even born.

"They're children," I argue.

Michael shrugs.

"What would I gain from it?"

Michael shrugs again.

"I don't even know where they are!"

"Oh, come on. You don't think it would be unreal to see them right now?" Michael suggests.

"That's not something I want to do." I'm pretty sure it ventures too close to violating one of those rules Blake mentioned, anyway.

Michael throws his hands up in defeat. "Fine, fine. Ignore my idea of fun. But there's something else we can do instead."

"I'm listening."

There's a glint in his eyes that could only be described as mischievous, and at this moment, I notice that his hands haven't left my shoulders. And I don't mind.

"Spend some time with me," he mutters, his voice low, like saying it too loudly will shatter the moment.

I study Michael's eyes—really study them. Boys are tricky beasts. Their words are like weasels that can wiggle their way into the smallest of cracks in another person's armor. When I came out as gay, my mother told me to watch out for them, for the way they can wrap around you and strangle what makes you special.

But that's not Michael. He's biting his bottom lip. His pulse, which I can feel in his thumbs, grows faster. His neck and his sharp clavicle become more pronounced as he swallows thickly.

Since I appeared here, I'd been out of my element, out of my time. But now, I held the power in my hands.

"I mean, where else would I go? It's not like I know anyone here. So the real question is, how are you going to make it up to me if this *perfect place* isn't actually perfect?"

———
———

Michael and I get two candy bars and Cokes from the corner store. It's not really a meal, but it's something, and the sugar feels like a rush of power and energy.

"Sorry, it's not much," Michael mutters as he chews.

"It's fine."

"I'm...low on cash. Journalism doesn't pay much, you know? We do it for the value of the free press, First Amendment, all that jazz."

"It's fine, Michael," I say, adding a reassuring smile. "This is great. Besides, who can ignore a Snickers bar? It really is perfect." And that's not a lie.

I'm starting to think that maybe, just maybe, even simple meals like this can be enjoyable with someone like Michael. He gives off that calming energy that I've heard people have. Unlike, as Isobel says, my frantic energy.

Maybe, in some ways, we complement each other in that sense.

"Speaking of jazz, your music, are you still playing?" I ask, refocusing my attention.

He smiles—no, beams—at me with pride. "You remember." It's more a statement of surprise than a question.

"Of course I do." It's only been a few days for me, but for him, it's been seven months. I wonder how much Michael has thought about me. Did he wonder if I was coming back? Did he start to think that I was a figment of his imagination?

"Yeah, I play a set downtown." He points in the general direction. "Once every two weeks. You should come by sometime."

Is that something I could do? I've never willingly time traveled to a specific period of time. But it should be possible. I doubt that Claire just throws herself through time and hopes for the best. I can learn how to do it.

"If you think, you know, that's something you'd want to do?" He nervously smiles. "You know, you don't have to, of course."

"Two weeks from now, yeah?"

"One week from this upcoming Saturday, actually, but yeah."

"What time?"

"Ten o'clock at the Citadel. Is that still around in your time?"

"Mm-hmm." It's a twenty-one-and-over club. But something tells me that getting in won't be a problem. "I'll be there," I promise.

His smile shifts from nervous to warm as we head deeper into the city. The streets are familiar, but not so familiar that this feels boring. Things have changed in the fifty years between Michael's time and mine. Side streets and one-way streets have been combined in my time and turned into two-way streets. Buildings have been demolished and ownership has changed. The city is still my city, but not completely.

And there's some comfort in that. The city is close enough to being my city but far enough away that at this moment, at this time with Michael? It's ours. It's not something that can be replicated by thousands of other...

What even are we?

"It's my turn for a question, I think," I say, breaking the silence.

Michael glances over at me, finishing the rest of his Coke.

He tosses it; the can makes a sharp sound as it hits the corner of the nearby trash can. It bounces once, twice, three times, and then lands inside it.

Michael doesn't think that I see the way he quietly fist-pumps, but I do.

"Shoot."

"What did you mean before when you said, 'It keeps me busy, which is good, since…'?"

"That's…not the question I thought you were going to ask."

I arch my brows incredulously.

"Who am I fooling? Of course you'd ask that."

I can tell from the stillness between us that the question is uncomfortable, prickly, even. It's jagged and cold, but it also burns hot at the same time.

"My parents aren't happy with me right now," he finally says. "They kicked me out. I'm working at that newspaper for room and board."

"They kicked you out because you're gay? Or because you want to be a musician?"

He shrugs. That's not an answer, but I don't think I'm going to get anything else out of him. Not yet, anyway.

We cross the street in silence. It's on me to say something; Michael's done pouring his heart out. But I don't know what to say. I've never dealt with something like that. When I came out, my parents were accepting. They love me for me, and my friends do too. I'm lucky—and rare. I know that. So stories about dealing with homophobia from parents? That's foreign to me.

But I can understand standing up for what you believe in and fighting for your own future, not the idea of a future someone else has for you. While we walk in silence, I try to play out what might happen if I told my parents that I'm not sure I want to go into medicine. They wouldn't kick me out, of course not, but they'd be disappointed. They'd question every choice I made and try to poke holes in my logic.

They'd be dismissive.

"You know you can't choose, right?" I finally say. "Being gay. It's not a choice."

"Is that what you boys in the future say? Science would beg to differ."

"Gayness being a disease isn't a scientific law, it's a theory," I remind him. "And theories can be proven wrong. I promise you, it gets better."

"Oh, I know it gets better. Just not here." He gestures around him. "Somewhere else... Somewhere like..."

"San Francisco?"

He laughs. "You think I'd want to go there? Why? Because I'm gay?"

"Is that such a bad reason? To go someplace where you'd be accepted?"

The history of society's treatment of gay people isn't something obscure. It sucked—that's how it can be summarized. My time, the twenty-first century, is the best time to be gay so far. But Michael doesn't know that because what he's living is all he knows.

A pang of guilt ripples through me. Is suggesting that he move breaking a rule? Am I using personal knowledge, knowledge that I've learned thanks to the hindsight of historians in my time period, in a way that violates one of the time travelers' creeds?

But, on the flip side, I'm doing it to help someone. That has to factor in, right?

I hold on to that and focus back on Michael.

"Plus, California is warmer."

"I don't want warmer," he objects. "I like Boston. I like that I know this city, that I know the people. The good, the bad, the ugly. It's all part of me."

"Well, how about New York? They say it's like Boston, just…"

"Dirtier?" he asks. "More expensive?"

"New York is more than that, and you wouldn't know if you didn't try. Staying somewhere just because you think it's what you're supposed to do or—"

"My parents kicked me out of the house, Dre."

Michael's interruption cuts deep, like a heated knife passing through flesh. It's a story as old as time, the gay kid kicked out of his house because his parents can't handle him being who he is.

Michael isn't ashamed; or at least, he doesn't show it. He holds his head up high. He leads us toward the Franklin Park Zoo, which isn't far. Signs cheerfully guide us toward our fauna adventure.

"That seems to me like even more of a reason for you to leave."

He shakes his head. "And let them win? No. Not a chance. I've built a life here; I've found a passion here, I have a family—a found family—here. I'm not leaving. And besides…"

But he doesn't finish, and even after I give him twenty seconds to continue, he still stays quiet.

"Besides what, Michael?"

"It's dumb."

"I should be the one to determine if it's dumb or not," I tease. "Come on, humor me. I traveled through time and space to see you."

"I didn't ask for that, you know."

"Yeah, but you'd miss me if I didn't."

"I know, I would," he says without hesitation. "Which is why I'm not sure I can leave. Or should leave. Because, if I do, who's to say you'll be able to find me again?"

The richness in Michael's words makes my own chest feel tight. There's no subtext, no lies, no misdirection. Just pure, simple honesty. This isn't some AP exam or SAT practice test. He really thinks that.

"You mean it, don't you?" I ask, though it's more of a statement.

Michael shrugs. "I don't want to break this connection that we have. I feel like we must have been meant to find each other. I don't want to throw away what the universe gave us. Is that so hard to believe?"

"No, not at all. It's just…"

Michael stops me, grabs my shoulders again, and forces me to look at him. His cheeks are rosy, and his breath is coming out in heavy white puffs. His nose is redder than the rest of his face, and his blue eyes look watery.

"Then let me be clear, Andre. I like you. I like you a lot, and I would rather stay here and spend two hours with you, wandering around a city, than a whole lifetime doing normal things that people expect of me. Normal is overrated, anyway."

This is it, I think. This is what people talk about in movies, in TV shows, in songs and books. That pit in your stomach that feels like a never-ending drop. That weightlessness that makes you dizzy but also makes you feel complete.

Hearing Michael say those words makes me feel all of those things at once.

Hearing Michael say those words confirms for me what I've been feeling this whole time.

That I feel the same.

"I…"

The air leaves my lungs. The earth swirls and rushes around me. Cold becomes warm. City streets become cherry wood floors. Outside becomes inside.

I hear music. Not the symphony of the city, but an Arctic Monkeys song playing in the room.

My head spins. Did I jump back on my own, or did something pull me back?

I steady myself by grabbing the couch, and Blake barely looks up. He's sitting on the couch, casually, both legs propped up on the table in front of him, holding a copy of *Sports Illustrated*—that damn smug smile on his face.

I feel a rush of emotions. Most of all, I'm upset that I left Michael at that moment, right when we were getting somewhere—although it scares me that I could have so much influence on his life.

But I also feel anger. Anger at how Blake forced me to jump. Anger because he doesn't seem to care what he just did.

"Okay," he says. "I can see you're mad."

"Oh, you picked up on that?" I growl, taking a step forward.

He stands up and takes a step back. "I should remind you, though, that I did what I did to prove a point."

"And what point is that?"

"Where did you go?" he asks.

"Does that matter? You *forced* me to jump, Blake!"

"I knew where you'd end up!"

"You knew or you *hoped* you knew?"

He opens his mouth, but no words come out. Quickly, he shuts his lips and his angled jaw makes them form a thin line.

"I was testing the tether theory," he argues, like that makes it better.

"What if I hadn't ended up next to Michael? There are plenty of places I could have gone that would have been *very* not cool for me. The nineteenth century! The early twentieth century! ANYTIME in the past for Black people!"

"You would have found your way back."

Anger turns white hot inside of me. I've never really understood what *seeing red* means. I'm not fully sure I do now. Because right now? I'm seeing white spots in front of my eyes.

"And what if I *didn't*? You're assuming that I would have, but it's pretty obvious that I *don't* know how to control it! I jumped because I was *startled*, and I jumped back because I was surprised!"

Was that even the right emotion? Doesn't matter.

"The point is," I continue, my voice shaking. "You...you... just assumed that you know what's best! And you know what? Maybe I have the wrong brother teaching me!"

The words come out of my mouth like venom, and I know, once I say them, that they were the wrong words. Not only because of the way Blake's eyes widen and then sharpen but also because of the bitterness they leave in my mouth, like I imagine cyanide would taste.

Some words are poison, and when you speak them, they might kill your target—and you along with it. Bringing up his dead brother like that, when I have his organ? That was a low blow.

"Get. Out," he says, punctuating each word like a sentence. "I mean it. Get out."

Part of me wants to apologize. I *should* apologize; that would be the right thing to do. But the stubborn part of me doesn't want to let him off the hook that easily. He doesn't get a pass. If he hadn't shoved me...

"I said get the hell out!"

I don't say anything. The rapid pulsing of my heart is enough to kick my body into high gear. I turn, walk out quickly, and slam the door behind me.

THIRTEEN

8:15 a.m.

ONE MISSED CALL: BLAKE MCINTYRE

9:15 a.m.

ONE MISSED CALL: BLAKE MCINTYRE

11:56 a.m.

ONE MISSED CALL: BLAKE MCINTYRE

It's been four days since my blowup with Blake, and in the past ninety-six hours, I've gotten nine calls and two voicemails from him. I'm not sure if that's something I should be proud of.

"You totally should be proud of it," Isobel had said during my self-imposed lunch break at the library. She drove halfway across town to meet me and bring me my favorite—a Philly cheesesteak.

Who said platonic love isn't as valuable as romantic love?

"I mean, come on," she scolded. "You have a boy from one of the most powerful families in Boston calling you. That means something."

After our first interaction with Mrs. McIntyre, Isobel did

her research. The McIntyres are a big philanthropic family, giving money to the symphony, education reform, mayoral campaigns, plenty of other political campaigns, and of course, medical research.

Mrs. McIntyre, at least on paper, is the one who has the money. She's from one of those old-money Boston families who came over on the *Mayflower* or something. Professionally, she's no slouch. She's a partner at McIntyre, Weston, and Grant, the best law firm in Massachusetts, one of the top three law firms on the East Coast, and one of the top five in the country.

Mr. McIntyre is no slouch either. Though not a power lawyer like his wife, he holds two PhDs, one in physics and one in biology. Rumor has it he was long-listed for a Noble Prize three years ago for his research regarding how time affects living organisms. Which, honestly, fits.

"You sure you don't want to know about the boys?" she asked. "I found some good dirt that you can use to your advantage. Knowledge is power, you know."

"I already put my foot in my mouth once. I don't need to do it again," I said and hugged her, promising to call her after my classes so we could hang out.

But instead of calling Isobel at four o'clock, all I can think about are the missed calls and voicemails from Blake. They're staring at me—taunting me—begging me to react.

"I should just delete them," I mutter, getting in my car and putting my book bag in the passenger seat. I have three classes worth of homework to do. I'm taking three yearlong classes crammed into six weeks. I don't have time to focus on anything else. Not Blake. Not time travel. Not Michael.

If I want to have any hope of graduating on time, of continuing my life and being me, this needs to be my priority.

Isn't that why I did all this? Why I fought so hard to survive? So I could have a normal life, or at least the chance at one.

Being a time traveler isn't normal.

Being associated with the richest, most powerful family in Boston isn't normal.

Traveling into the past to date someone isn't normal.

And yet, with all that truth staring me in the face, I still press Call Back on my phone.

Ring.

Maybe I should hang up.

Ring. Ring.

The truth is, our argument? It wasn't completely his fault. Ignoring him is passive-aggressive, and I know this. But that doesn't stop me from feeling—white-hot rage. It's the way he turned the tables on *me*; he pushed *me* into the past, and then, somehow, he makes it about him and how *I* was wrong?

Ring. Ring. Ring.

I should hang up. I shouldn't give him a second chance. I should tell Claire that I want her to teach me how—

"Andre?"

Blake's deep voice catches me off guard. There's a hint of discomfort in it, too, an upward inflection that makes him seem softer, less in control than usual.

"You there?" he asks.

"Yeah. Hey," I say, after a beat.

"Hey."

The clouds are turning a darker gray more quickly than I expected. Soft droplets of rain pat against my windshield. It's going to get humid quickly. And my car doesn't have AC. Great.

Who should speak first? Should it be me?

He did reach out first. He made the first move by calling. The ball's technically in my court.

Screw it.

"Look, I'm—"

"I'm—"

We both speak at the same time, then we both fall quiet at the same time too.

"You go first," he says.

"No, you," I suggest. "When I lead a conversation, it tends to go off the rails."

A soft chuckle comes out of Blake's mouth. Finally, after seconds passing, he speaks.

"Can you come over? Just for a little bit? I want to apologize."

I pull my phone away from my face to check the time— 4:15. Mom and Dad will be home around 6:00. It'll take twenty minutes to get to Blake's. I can stay for an hour, and then head home. Make up some excuse about how I was studying or hanging out with Isobel, who'll cover for—

Shit. Isobel.

I promised I'd hang with her today. We've barely hung out

at all since I got back from the hospital, except for the time we went to visit Blake's house, and that could barely be classified as a hangout session. I *promised* her, and knowing Izzy, she probably has a whole evening planned.

But this is more important. I'd be a fool to think, even for a moment, that I could just let the world of time travel and all its possibilities slip through my fingers.

"Andre?" Blake asks again.

"Heading your way now."

I hang up without another word and send a quick text to Izzy, then throw my phone onto the seat next to me. As I drive, it vibrates, and I know exactly what her reply is going to say.

FOURTEEN

When I arrive at Blake's house and let him know I'm there, he sends a text back before I can get out of the car.

Door's open. Come on up the stairs.

First door on the right.

"Not ominous at all," I mutter. Sure enough, the door is unlocked, and the house looks exactly how it did four days ago. Everything perfectly in its place. Devoid of any sort of real warmth. More like a mausoleum than a house.

I take the steps two at a time and follow Blake's instructions. Sure enough, he's sitting there in his room, and music is playing from his stereo.

"Cardinal Planes?" I ask, pointing to the system.

He nods, looking down at a photo that he's holding in his hand. I can't make out what's inside the wooden frame, but I can guess.

"Dave took me to see them when I was fifteen. Mom and Dad were more focused on me passing algebra, but Dave argued that it was important to have fun and let loose every once in a while. He drove down from Harvard at eight o'clock one night when Mom and Dad were working late, picked me up, and took me to the concert."

"Their first Boston concert? I heard it was a once-in-a-lifetime show."

The corner of his cheek rises in a grin. "Yeah, it was." Blake gently puts the photograph down and stands, dressed in a pair of joggers and a well-fitted T-shirt. He rocks back and forth on his heels, hands shoved into his pockets. He looks smaller than me, even though that's not the case. Blake's easily three inches taller.

He breathes out, speaking his whole sentence like one word. "I shouldn't have pushed you like I did, just to test you. Especially before you were ready."

"And?"

"And that was…a shitty thing to do?"

I want to reply with something sarcastic. *No shit*, perhaps. But I bite my tongue.

"You suck at saying sorry, you know," I say, keeping my voice light so he won't take it too personally. "Didn't your parents ever teach you the components of a good apology?"

Before he can answer, I bridge the space between us and push him back so that his knees buckle and he sits back down in his chair.

"An apology has three parts—" I begin.

"You're serious?" Blake asks. "Oh my God, you are serious."

"The first: I'm sorry. The second: what you are sorry for.

And finally: how you are going to do better next time. So let's try that again."

Blake narrows his eyes, studying me for any cracks that he can exploit. But he won't find any.

"I'm serious," I urge. "This will help you in the long run. Help you be a better person. You're teaching me time travel; I'm teaching you basic life manners. Call it payment in kind."

"You still want to work with me?"

"Should I not?" Now I'm thinking I shouldn't.

But before either of us can speak, the front door opens.

"Blake?" Claire calls. "I know you're here! I saw your car. Is that Andre's I saw too?"

Blake and I look at each other, his surprised expression mirroring my own. He gestures silently to me— *Talk*.

"Yeah," I choke out. "Mrs. McIntyre, it's me."

"Good! Are you free to stay for dinner? I insist! Come down and help me, will you?"

She doesn't ask again or wait for me to confirm. Instead, I hear the soft sounds of jazz music flow through the speakers in the house.

"Who is this?" I ask. "Playing?"

"*Juju* by Wayne Shorter, I think," Blake answers. "One of my dad's favorite composers. Why, you into jazz?"

A smile creeps onto my face that I do my best to hide. I shake my head and leave, heading down the stairs two at a time.

I hurry down the stairs and follow the sound of running water, the sweet smell of burning butter, and the heat that breaks through the blanket of chill that the AC provides. In the kitchen, Claire is leaning over the counter and reading a recipe, her brow furrowed.

"How are you with cooking?" she asks without looking up.

"Decent. I can make a mean set of waffles and eggs."

The right corner of her mouth lifts into a smile, and she points to a pot. "Want to man the mashed potatoes for me?"

"Sure."

Is this what she wanted? A cooking partner? Why not ask Blake?

"Just keep stirring them until they are thick," she instructs.

I listen, staring at the bubbling off-white substance like it has secrets to tell me. Mom doesn't allow me in the kitchen whenever she's trying to perfect even the simplest of recipes, which is kind of hilarious considering she usually fails and ends up ordering takeout. Even though she's bad at it, she cooks to feel calmer, and my father and me being in the kitchen doesn't help her relax.

But she's taught me a few tricks, enough so that when I go to college, I won't be one of those kids who eats Pop Tarts and pizza bites for every meal.

"Can I add something to it?" I ask.

Claire sucks on her finger when she looks at me and nods.

I move through the kitchen, searching for what I need, finding the paprika and cayenne pepper. I fold them into the fluffy whites, adjusting the percentages depending on my taste. I want to ask her *Why Blake?* to settle my burning urge for knowledge once and for all. Cut the snake's head off before it multiplies.

"When did you find out you were a time traveler?" I ask instead.

Claire doesn't stop stirring the concoction that she's creating, but a smile does appear on her lips.

"How old are you, Andre? Seventeen?"

"Eighteen in six months."

"So you're a December baby. Just like me." She beams proudly. "Then I was about ten years younger than you when I first jumped."

She pours the mixture into the pot. It sizzles, and the air fills with aromatic smells of chives, onions, and peppers.

"I was obsessed with history as a kid, you see. A double-edged sword for a time traveler. The *desire* to learn about someplace is sometimes enough to *actually* make you jump. And for me, that was Paris, two weeks before the Germans invaded."

I whistle, loud and sharp. She nods. "It was a jarring experience. But that's what I think makes us so fortunate, Andre. We get to see history firsthand. Explore parts of it that have been excluded by the victors or get front-row seats to the biggest, most important events. It's a luxury and a blessing."

"And a curse," I add, putting the dish in the oven.

"This again?"

"It's one thing to be able to look back at history with twenty-twenty hindsight and think, *I would have done this differently if I were there*, but to actually *be* there and do nothing? Doesn't that make us worse than the people who can't do anything?"

Without missing a beat, as if she had been waiting for me to step right into that trap and come to that conclusion, she responds. "Rule number three," she reminds me. "We can't change the past."

"Because why?" I object.

"Because there's no almanac that can tell us how one change will affect the rest of the world. What if we stopped a bomber from destroying a building, but instead he bombs a stadium?"

"Or what if because you stopped the bomber, someone inside that building lives and is able to find a cure for cancer?" I counter.

"We can't make a concrete choice in the hopes of an abstract solution, Andre."

"That's exactly what science is."

"We can agree to disagree on that topic."

The room falls silent as she continues to prepare dinner. I busy myself, getting what she needs when she asks for it, trying to predict what she will need before she has to ask. We continue this standstill, this awkward dance, for about ten minutes.

"How is being taught by my son working out for you?" she asks, looking up as she sifts some flour into a bowl. "He's not going too fast, is he?"

"We only started the basics," I explain. "Rules, regulations, the boring stuff of time travel."

"But important." She points a wooden spoon at me. Flour mixed with eggs threatens to drip off. "Those rules are there for your—and every time traveler's—protection, Andre."

"You sound like my parents."

"Then they must be very wise, and I hope to meet them someday. Reach into the fridge and get me the bacon, will you?"

I follow through, getting the three-pound bag of bacon. "Can I ask you a question?"

"Of course. But work on chopping that up while you do."

"How did you know?" I ask. "That I time traveled the first time. You said you felt it. How?"

Claire doesn't stop stirring her pot, but from my side view, I can see the playful, teasing smile on her lips. "This is probably not the answer you want to hear, but some things in the world cannot yet be explained by science. They just are."

"That sounds like magic," I say. "You're using the fallback of magic as your answer?"

"Not magic," she clarifies. "Just…not yet explained."

I'm not happy with that answer. It feels like a cop-out. Is it so hard for people to say, *I don't know*? And if they actually do know, why keep it hidden?

Instead, I steer the conversation in another direction.

"Are there others like me? I mean, I got the ability to travel from David's liver, and his other organs went to other people, right? Did they also gain the same ability?"

"David's other organs were damaged in the accident."

"So I'm the only one?" I ask.

"Yes, and I'm glad for it. Your passion for knowledge, your stubbornness... Those things make you an excellent time traveler."

I'm not sure if that answer satisfies me, but it's enough for now.

I hear Blake's heavy footsteps before I hear his voice. He comes down the staircase and rounds the corner, now dressed in a worn Yale shirt with the *Y* half faded off. Casually, he walks into the kitchen and kisses his mom's cheek. He makes all the right motions, and she responds in kind: a tilt of the head, a small smile. But everything looks and feels so...mechanical. The actions are there. The emotion is not.

"I'm making dessert, but dinner should be ready in just a few minutes. Blake, can you help Andre set the table?"

"Is Dad going to join us?"

Claire is in the middle of answering when the front door opens once again. Unlike before, though, the energy is different. Claire gives off an air of sophistication and poise. Greg, when he enters, is like a hurricane of papers and anxious energy.

"Did I miss it?"

"Still cooking, dear."

"Oh, thank God."

Greg lets out a breath, and the level of anxiety in the room lowers as he starts putting his things down.

"Andre." He smiles, nodding to me. "Nice to see you again. Hey," he says, turning to Blake. "How was your—"

Blake snorts under his breath, grabs a handful of utensils and napkins, and gives them to me, completely ignoring his father.

"You like iced tea?" he asks me. "I'm going to get the glasses. Do you know how to set the table?"

He's tenser than he was upstairs, I think. His shoulders are tight. Is his relationship with his parents really that bad? Does just being around them feel like being close to the Elephant's Foot of Chernobyl?

"I'm from the other side of town; I'm not uneducated."

Blake opens his mouth to say something, probably some witty rebuttal, but instead he shuts it tight. He puts the pitcher down, with only two glasses filled.

"Call me when dinner's ready."

He walks by me, heading back up the stairs before Claire can stop him. She sighs and turns to me with a weary smile.

"That was a joke," I tell her. "It wasn't meant to be rude."

"I know, dear."

"You just stepped into a hornet's nest and had no idea," Greg says with an apologetic smile. "He'll get better."

But I'm not sure if he's saying that more to reassure me or himself.

"That doesn't sound very convincing."

Claire shrugs, putting the finished mashed potatoes in a bowl. "You'll see," she says, disappearing into the living room.

Again, not at all convincing.

FIFTEEN

"Andre? Can you join me in my study for a second?"

I'm halfway through setting the table when Mr. McIntyre pokes his head in from the adjoining room.

"It'll just take a moment."

Will it, though?

I peek into the kitchen. It looks like Mrs. McIntyre is almost done.

I walk through the living room again and slide into Greg's study. It's massive—so big that I think, if we lived here, Mom might divorce Dad to have it to herself. Hell, Dad might divorce Mom for it. It's lined with about three times as many books as the living room and has three desks with papers, maps, and other documents scattered around. Greg reminds me of an archetype I know far too well: the absentminded professor.

This, I can relate to.

"What do you teach?" I ask, idly picking up one of the papers. It's written in sloppy Arabic, which I'm guessing is his own writing. "My parents are professors at Boston College and

Northeastern, both in the sciences. Well, both in STEM. Mom's in statistics, and Dad, biology."

He glances over for a brief moment, adjusting his glasses in the same way my dad does. "Really now? I knew there was something I liked about you. Your parents must be smart. Linguistics, for me; I'm the department chair at Harvard. I specialize in dead languages."

"I'm guessing being a time traveler helps with that?" I venture. "Being able to go back to when they spoke it, and hearing it firsthand?"

Greg chuckles, stacking some papers and dropping them into a file drawer. "It did, at one point. I stopped being able to travel in my twenties. Not much older than you are now, actually." There's a darkness in his eyes when he says that. Not anger or resentment, but sorrow. Like he's lost an old friend.

"So, Andre. I'm sorry we didn't get to talk more when you first came to visit."

"Mrs. McIntyre was more than accommodating, Mr. McIntyre."

"Please." He gently raises his hand. "Call me Greg. You're practically family now."

We both know how awkward that sounds as soon as it leaves his lips. But while I avert my gaze, he does his best to backtrack.

"Because you're a time traveler," he adds quickly. "We call each other family."

Not because I have your son's organ inside of me?

"I got you."

The awkwardness is heavy in the air for half a minute before I decide to break it.

"I want to say it again, Mr.—Greg."

Greg's brow furrows.

"To say thank you." I gesture to my abdomen. "For giving me this. For saving my life. I know it probably—"

Greg holds his hand up again. But this time, he doesn't speak. He shuffles past me, squats down, and opens a box. He sifts through it, pulling out folders and books and carefully stacking them until he finds what he wants. Using his palm, he slowly, carefully wipes it clean and passes it to me.

Another photo album. "David was always helping people. It's all he wanted to do in his life. In fact, he didn't care about being able to time travel, because he couldn't fix the wrongs of the past.

"That said, the fact that you have his organ, is, in a sense, David doing what he always wanted to do. Helping someone. I know, deep down, that this is what David was always destined to do. Help. And he'll help you every day. He found a purpose in a way that some—most—people never do. And I couldn't be prouder.

"So..." He hurries back to his chair and sits down, resting his elbows on his knees. "Tell me everything about you. Your passions, what you like, your schooling, where you want to go to college, if you want to go to college, what you want to do when you grow up. As little or as much as you're willing to tell me. I want to know. I like to know everything about my friends and those who might one day be part of my family."

If some random man came up to me and asked me to tell him everything about me because he wanted to be friends, I'd probably kick him in the balls and run in the opposite direction.

But Greg McIntyre isn't a random man. He's a man grieving the loss of his son in the only way he knows how: talking to the one connection to his dead child. And perhaps in some twisted, deep-down, backward way, he feels guilty. Maybe he hasn't had time to grieve yet.

But I can help ease that grief, and as Greg said, David only ever wanted to help people.

Maybe I can take a bit of that burden, of that life mission, and help someone right now.

And so I sit down and tell him everything that makes me *me*.

Dinner with the McIntyres isn't nearly as uncomfortable as I thought it would be. And the food isn't bad either.

"Cooking is how I de-stress," Claire says, dabbing at the corners of her mouth. Somehow, her bright red lipstick is still impeccable. "Between the firm, the hospital, the PTA…"

"We get it, Mom, you do a lot," Blake says with food in his mouth. Greg glares at his son, who mumbles an apology under his breath.

While this whole interaction goes down, I sneak a look at my phone, where I see a series of texts from Isobel.

Your parents are wondering

where you are.

I lied for you, by the way, but

where are you?

Oh my God, you're at her house

again, aren't you?

I stg if you're dead, Dre, I'm going

to kill her myself.

"So tell me, Andre," Claire says. "How was your first jump?"

"Sorry?" I ask, putting my phone away.

She flourishes her hands excitedly. "It's a rite of passage for a traveler. Everyone remembers theirs. It tells a lot about a person. I already told you mine." She takes a sip of her wine and gestures to Greg, who jumps in without a second thought.

"Egypt, when Cleopatra became ruler," Greg notes. "I was in the crowd. Completely scared shitless."

"*Greg!*"

"Excuse my French."

"And you?" I turn to Blake. "I know you can't jump, but I'm sure you've thought about it, right?" I ask. Mostly, my hope is to get Blake to contribute to the conversation. To make up for my earlier faux pas and crack that hard shell.

It seems that asking that question was not the way to do it.

Blake slams his fork down on his plate, loudly enough for a sharp note to ripple through the air and direct everyone's attention to him.

Claire glances over at her son, only moving her eyes, before looking at me.

"I want to make one thing clear," Blake says slowly. "Just because I can't jump, that doesn't make me less than anyone at this table, all right?"

"No one was saying that, dear," Claire chimes in. "Yes, you being unable to jump is—"

"If you say it's a goddamned travesty, Mom, I swear to fucking God."

"Hey," Greg booms. "Don't talk to your mother that way, especially at the dinner table, especially in front of a guest."

Blake shuts his mouth, but I can't tell if it's out of respect or self-preservation. He chews quickly, stabbing his food with the utmost deliberation.

Finally, I break the silence. "It was good," I say, clearing my throat. "You asked about my first jump? I went back to the sixties. End of the sixties, actually."

"Oh, that's a good time," she says, her face beaming with approval. I can't help but wonder what her reaction would have been if I'd said, like, the Ice Age. A frown?

Claire puts her fork and knife down, crossing them over each other on the plate. She rests her chin in the palm of her right hand and leans forward, her eyes *actually smizing.*

"Did you go to a disco? Oh! Please tell me you did something amazing! You can't get your first jump back, Andre!"

"Well, then couldn't you argue that no matter what I did, it was memorable? I mean, most people don't time travel."

Claire pauses and blinks owlishly at me, like she's processing.

Greg chuckles. "He's got you there, babe!"

I smile and look over at Blake. Maybe he finds this funny too. Maybe he's processed his uncomfortable tenseness.

No such luck.

The only one not having a good time is Blake, who is still scowling.

I try to silently say something to him, make a mental check-in through eye contact, but he doesn't look up from his plate. He's just moving around the same goddamned pea he's been pushing with his fork for the last five minutes.

I didn't do anything wrong, I tell myself.

So why do I feel like his bad mood is my cross to bear?

"What are you planning on studying, Andre?" Greg asks.

"I want to do biology," I reply without thinking about it. It's such an automatic response—telling people that I'm going to cure some disease, or try to. This is the first time ever that the words don't feel right against my tongue, and it takes me a moment to figure out why.

Michael.

The seeds of doubt that he placed in my head are taking root. I can hear his echoing voice playing devil's advocate in favor of me finding my own path, finding my passion.

What a dumb thing, passion. Passion comes from what you put your blood, sweat, and tears into. Passion is what you do on the side when you're done with the job that gives you the freedom to explore things. Passion, and following it, is a white middle-class concept, not a Black middle-class one.

"I think I want to study oncology." I force the words out. They create a sense of responsibility. Now the McIntyres will know me as That Black Kid Who Wants to Cure Cancer. I can't let them down. I have to follow through with it.

A flimsy stunt of mental gymnastics, but it'll hold.

Greg nods proudly and nudges Blake. "See? That's the type of person you need to be. Someone with an idea and the direction to realize it."

Blake's shoulders tense, as do mine. We all know this won't end well. Especially when Greg says, "Lacrosse isn't an end goal, Blake. It's something you do to pass the time."

And that's when the geyser known as Blake McIntyre explodes.

Blake hits the table hard enough that his glass of iced tea tilts and spills everywhere, dripping onto the floor. He stands, pushing the chair out from behind him until it collides with the wall.

"Look, I'm sorry I'm not Dave. I'm sorry he's the one who died and not me. Trust me—I know you would have preferred that, Dad."

"That's not—"

"But I'm here. And you know what? You and Mom are going to have to deal with it. Taking it out on me? Not cool. I'm here. I'm alive. How about focusing on that instead of trying to mold me into your other son?"

Blake storms off before his parents can respond, leaving all three of us dumbstruck. Claire sighs heavily.

"You need to apologize, Greg," she warns, throwing her napkin down, but not before quickly dabbing at the corners of her mouth. "Now."

"I'm not going to apologize to him. He should know that he doesn't get to treat us all like emotional punching bags. He's not the only one hurting."

"That's not the point, and you know it!"

"Then what is the point?"

"He's our son!"

The argument continues to escalate, and with each rising voice, I feel smaller. Blake's somewhere upstairs, and I should probably follow him, but I can't help but feel like there's a part of this argument that's my fault.

Since the first time I visited the McIntyres and saw their family dynamics, something has always felt off. It's like they are all magnets of the same pole, trying to push themselves together when, logically, they never could. And, finally, the force they've been exerting on each other backfired and blew them apart.

This argument was the manifestation of anger, pain, and regrets that are all umbrellaed under one word.

Grief.

That's what all this is. Grief that's bubbling under the surface. No one here wants to talk about what happened...which I still don't fully understand. Ignoring the situation won't solve it, but that's easy to say as an outsider looking in. Would Dad and I talk if Mom died? Would Mom and I discuss it if Dad got hit by a car on his way home? Would Mom and Dad talk if I suddenly collapsed right now and died before getting to the hospital?

No. Yes. No.

The yelling continues, but I do my best to push it out.

If Blake is right, then all I need to do is think about Michael to transport myself to him. I don't need to be here; I can be anywhere. So why not take advantage of that?

I conjure up an image of Michael, and I hold on to that thought. His height. His arms. His hair. His smile. How he smells. Him playing music. The Citadel. My process.

Visualize it. Every inch. Let it bleed into all of your—

"Well, look what the cat dragged in."

SIXTEEN

Wherever we are, it's not where I would've expected us to be.

The last few times I've jumped to meet Michael, we've been somewhere familiar—somewhere isolated. Like the only people who matter are him and me.

Wherever we are now is dingy, and the air is thick with the smell of alcohol, sweat, and smoke. Perspiration trickles down my neck and my forehead too. It's a very specific feeling, the stickiness and the invasion of one's personal space. It's a sense and feeling that I can pinpoint to one location.

The Citadel.

But none of it seems to affect Michael. He's smiling, like he always does, but this time, it's a wider grin, like what you'd see on a family member who has just learned that someone they love is still alive.

"I did it," I whisper to myself.

He arches a brow but doesn't ask any questions. "Still as strange as always, Andre Cobb from Boston. We really need to stop meeting like this." He scolds me but still wraps his arms around me tightly. The smell of alcohol is strong on him, along with the smell of cologne and smoke and sweat, but all of it comes together to make the Michael I know and love.

And I didn't realize how much I missed it. How much I *love* those smells.

I wrap my arms around him, holding him close, like his molecules might slip through my fingers in that very moment. When we pull back, I'm the first one to speak.

"You're playing here tonight, yeah?"

He nods. "That's why you came, right?"

"If I say no, will I lose my brownie points?"

"Nothing can lose you points with me. Come on, sit, sit."

I follow him, weaving through the room, which smells like the thick of bodies, and sit at a circular table about ten feet from the stage. There's a pair of twins riffing off each other, like two athletes playing vocal Ping-Pong. It's majestic, impressive, and a skill I'll never have.

Michael taps his finger slowly against the table in beat with the two. He's focused on them, his lips moving rapidly, like he's whispering some incantation under his breath. Or a curse. A twinge of jealousy spikes through my body.

I've just traveled through time and space for him, and he's solely focused on his music. Seeing him focused like that is attractive. There's something different about Michael's passion for music than other people's. Maybe because I know what he's been through to get here. Maybe because I know what he's sacrificed. I'm not sure. But this feels like he deserves this moment, where nothing else but the music matters.

When the duo stops, the crowd erupts in jovial glee. People stand, hooting and hollering, sending a sharp note through the air. Once the crowd calms down, the noise in the room is nothing louder than a murmur. I notice, as Michael takes a long sip of his beer, that there's a guitar next to him, taking up a seat.

"What are you going to play?"

"That's the question you have?" he replies. "Usually you're asking, *What year is it?*"

"Thought I would shake it up this time," I tease.

"I appreciate that." A beat, or rather another swig of beer, passes. "Saturday," he finally says, looking over at me. "You've only been gone a few days. I'm not even sure if *gone* is the right word. *Missing* sounds better."

"I knew where I was," I remind him. "I was back home—in my time."

Michael shakes his head, pushing the beer over to me and offering me a swig, which I take—begrudgingly. "Not what I meant," he says. He pauses, then adds, "*I* missed you."

Michael must know that I'm mentally freaking out. His rough hand squeezes my shoulder just once. His breath, warm and sweet-smelling, tickles my ear.

"Trust me," he whispers.

His words feel like some sort of Russian activation code, because as soon as I hear them, my shoulders relax, I nod, and my heart slows down. Michael sits there with me, in the faint neon light, submerged in the smells of peanuts and bad beer, his eyes locked with mine.

"You okay?" he finally asks.

My throat feels dry, and all I can do is nod. But that's enough. He leads me over to the bar for a drink, and I notice, for the first time, where we are.

It's mostly filled with men, but the dim neon lights give it an eerie, sunset-like glow, which makes it hard to see clearly. It's relatively quiet; the conversations are barely above a low murmur, even though the alcohol seems to be flowing. Michael's at home. His body is relaxed as he chats with the bald bartender with strong, bloated pecs and triceps. And then it hits me.

The Citadel is a gay jazz club.

I quickly flip through the history I remember for 1970. Gay rights weren't a huge thing, but they were starting to gain traction, thanks to the Stonewall riots a few months prior. But there was also a war going on. Vietnam. All of these men look draft age.

So why weren't they there?

"You're wondering the same thing I wondered the first time I came here," Michael says, slipping me a glass of beer filled to the brim. By the time I look up, Michael's already halfway through his own massive glass. When he sets it down, there's a film of white on his top lip, making his mustache look like a salt-and-pepper one.

"College," he explains. "Deferment. I'm sure you know all about that, yeah?"

"We don't have the draft anymore," I say, using my thumb to clean his face. His blue eyes cross, focusing on my thumb, then settle on my face, watching me, not my finger, until I'm done. "But I do know about it."

"Because this war is a freakin' shit show," a man slurs next to Michael. He's wearing a jacket, military issued, but I can't tell what the patches and letters mean.

I do know what the missing right arm means. I want to tell him, *Thank you for your service*, or something, but the words don't come out. It's like I feel embarrassed to say something like that to a veteran. Or maybe it's because I know that his sacrifice, in the greater picture, didn't stop anything.

"Damn straight, Johnny," Michael says, patting his back. Johnny grumbles, brushing off Michael's hand. When a waiter in a tight shirt walks by, Michael taps his thigh and juts his head toward Johnny. "His drinks are on me."

"You got it, sugar."

Michael turns back to me. "It's exactly like Johnny said. This war is a mess. It's obvious that it's going to go down in history as the most fucked-up war ever. I don't even have to be a time traveler to know that."

Michael mutters the second half of that statement around the rim of his glass, grinning.

"What?" I ask.

Michael shrugs, nodding to my glass. He raises his hand, brushing hair out of his way. "Not a fan of beer?"

"You could say that." I remember all the literature about

drinking after a transplant. I've already been pushing my luck with the other drinks I had with Michael. Plus, he's right, beer isn't my favorite thing in the world. I hate the sour taste it has.

"Oh, so now you're being picky?" he teases, nudging me with his shoulder.

"I'm not in the mood for this, Michael."

The words come out far harsher than I intend them to, and the way that Michael pulls away and his shoulders tense tells me that he agrees. I sigh, staring at the brown liquid. You only live once, right? A few sips won't hurt me.

With that, I grab it and take a long drink. It tastes like... yeast, bubbly yeast, but I stomach about three gulps of it. I set it down, wiping my mouth with my arm, and gulp down half the cup of tap water that was put in front of me. Before I can put the glass down, Michael pats my back—hard. Hard enough for water to spill on the front of my pants. That stupid grin, wide and boyish, is painted all over his face.

"See? That wasn't so bad, was it?"

"Absolutely awful."

"Now you're just playing hard to get."

"There's nothing for you to get here."

"Oh, just you wait, Andre. You and I aren't even playing the same game, and you've already lost."

Normally, if I heard someone say that, I'd call them a creep. But when Michael says it, his features soften. He's teasing.

"How did we get in here, anyway?" I say, clearing my throat and forcing another sip of beer.

"No one's going to ask your age. You look older than you are. And no one really cares here." Michael stops mid-sip, hastily putting his drink down. His eyes widen as he studies me, leaning in close, so close that I can smell the beer on his breath and his cologne.

"You're telling the truth, aren't you? About the draft?" he asks, pulling back. "Has anything else changed that I need to be concerned about?"

"We're always going to be in a war of some sort. So just get ready for that."

He groans, thumping his forehead against the table.

I flourish my hands, taking a fake bow. "Welcome to America, the land of the free and the home of hypocrisy."

"Hear! Hear!" he replies, raising his glass, which sloshes beer onto him. He yelps and jumps, and his shirt and denim jacket are stained. "Shit!" he yells.

I quickly grab any napkins I can, patting him down. The napkins absorb a lot of the beer, but his shirt's still damp.

"This is all your fault, you know."

"How is this *my* fault?" I protest. "You spilled the drink."

"You made me laugh!"

"I made a factual statement about our country! You cheered."

"I know when to recognize and appreciate wisdom. What can I say?"

I stop with my hands on his pecs, looking up at Michael. When our eyes meet, he's smiling an easy, open smile, strands of dirty-blond hair in front of his blue eyes. It's a sight to behold, a dizzying image.

"You did this on purpose, didn't you?"

Michael scoffs.

"I think you spilled that beer on purpose so that I would touch you."

It sounds stupid when I say it out loud, and I clamp my lips tight to stop myself from saying anything else outrageous.

But Michael doesn't seem to care. In fact, he acts more like a moth to a flame, attracted by my words, and takes a step forward, and then another. By the time he stops, he's very much in my personal space, and my back is against the table. He places his hands against each side of me, and even with him so close, I can't smell his beer, his cologne, or anything.

It's because I'm not breathing.

Everything melts away as he leans in. The world behind him blurs into a black and faint neon nothingness. His lips brush against my ear as he whispers, "If I wanted your hands on me, trust me, it wouldn't be at a bar."

He pulls back once again, still close, our thighs touching, his eyes locked with mine.

This isn't how I thought my first kiss would go. But we don't always get to choose who we fall in love with. Sometimes we just have to take a leap of faith and be comfortable with things not going according to plan. I, more than anyone, should understand that.

Do I want Michael to kiss me? I think so. Do I want my first kiss to be with him? Probably. But should we do it here?

As Michael leans forward, I don't stop him. I don't move closer either. This is it. The moment I've seen on TV, heard Isobel talk about, watched porn about—this moment right here. A kiss. My heart thumps loudly in my chest, so loudly that I barely hear the MC on stage.

"Up next we have a regular here; Michael Gray is going to perform a song for us. Give him a good ol' Citadel welcome, will ya?"

Michael stops, an inch or so from my mouth. The smell of beer doesn't bother me anymore.

"Damn it," he whispers, pulling back and grabbing his guitar. "To be continued. Be here when I return?" he asks, taking off his jacket, revealing a sleeveless black fitted T-shirt.

"Where else would I go?"

"I dunno, the future, maybe?"

"Rule number one of time traveling: no traveling to the future."

He quirks a brow, waves me off, and heads onto the stage. He's almost sitting down when he rests his guitar against the stool and quickly runs back to our table. I grab his beer, thinking that's what he wants, but before I raise it, he quickly presses his lips against mine.

"Be right back," he whispers as the crowd is hooting and hollering. If my heart was beating fast before, it feels like it's going to jump out of my chest now.

Michael Gray just kissed me.

Michael Gray just kissed me.

Michael Gray just freakin' kissed me!

I repeat it over and over again in my head until it sinks in. Once it does, Michael's situated on the stool. Cool, calm, and collected, he speaks softly into the microphone.

"This song is for a guy I've only known for a few days, but it feels like I've known him forever," he says, his eyes on me the whole time.

And in that moment, as he plays, for what feels like the first time since I started traveling, nothing really matters.

SEVENTEEN

If I thought talking with Michael before was easy, walking through the city with him after the kiss is a cakewalk.

I remember when I had my first crush on someone at school, I asked my mom how I would know if they were the one or not. She didn't take it seriously; who would take the crush of a twelve-year-old seriously? But she did give me advice that I've thought about for a while.

"When you know they're the one, you'll know because you'll be able to sit peacefully in silence with them, without it being a problem. You'll be able to know what they are thinking without having to ask them, and they'll be able to do the same with you. But most of all, the simple problems, the small problems that bother you about most people? With that person, they don't bother you. That's what the right person does for you, Dre. And I hope, one day, you'll find them."

I don't know if Michael's that person, but I know he fits all those categories.

I know we've been walking for four blocks, without saying

a single word, and that's okay. I know when he wants to turn, he only has to give the gentlest tug before my body responds in kind.

Until, suddenly, he decides it's time to speak.

"So about that kiss."

I need to pick my words carefully. Isobel always says that, in these moments, how you react to a boy can determine how the relationship moves forward. Who has the power? Is it equal? Is it push and pull? Don't play too hard to get, but don't cave just because he kissed you.

"What about it?"

Michael shrugs. "Did you like it?"

Another pause. Honesty or muted emotion? Honesty or muted emotion? Honesty or...

"Yeah," I say, quietly, then I clear my throat and add, "I liked it a lot. And your music too."

Michael turns his head away from me, his cheeks a faint red. I can't tell if it's from him blushing or from the cold, but either way, the rosiness and bashfulness look good on him.

And a part of me, a large part of me, wants to see that blush again.

"Yeah?" he asks.

"It was amazing," I reply.

He gives a fake, over-the-top bow. "Got some experience?"

I quirk a brow, and a smile creeps around the edges of my lips. "Is that your way of asking if I have a boyfriend?"

"In so many words, yes."

"No, I don't." I pause again. "Do you?"

He shakes his head.

"Not so easy, you know? I mean, yeah, I'm out, and I'm happy I'm gay, but still." He shrugs. "My parents don't want this. The world doesn't want me to be happy. Having a boyfriend... That feels like a dream."

I catch myself before saying, *A guy like you could get any guy you want*. Because, yes, Michael is hot—very, very hot in that River Phoenix type of way. But it's harder in the seventies for gay people. In most U.S. states, it's illegal to be gay. AIDS is going to be a thing soon. Gay people aren't on TV, and when they are, *if* they are, it's always negative rep.

I'm lucky. It's easier for me. It's not perfect, sure. But I have rights. I don't have to be closeted. There are people in my generation who *still* deal with that. I don't think I've ever thought about how privileged and lucky I really am.

"Well, that's good for both of us, isn't it?" I say, focusing back on Michael. "Means you're not a cheater."

"And you're not a home wrecker."

"Good."

"Good."

Silence falls over us again, a comfortable silence. I'm not sure what part of Boston we're in; the nighttime, fifty years of history, and the blanket of white snow make it harder to pinpoint any specific time or place. But I suppose it doesn't matter, because being with Michael, I could be in 2021 or 1719, and I'd still be happy.

Actually, I'd be truly happy.

"I'm sorry, by the way." Michael's voice cuts through the silence. "When I questioned whether you were just following your parents' desire for you to be a doctor or your own? That was wrong of me. Everyone should be free to be who they want to be."

"You remember that?" I ask.

He nods. "I thought about it a lot, actually. How wrong it was of me to attack you like that."

We pass by Faneuil Hall, the marketplace and meeting hall located near the waterfront and Government Center. I think about how in 1960 it was designated a National Historic Landmark. Just ten years ago, this place became solidified as an essential part of Boston history. For a moment, I wonder if I can jump back there, to see that moment and create my own scrapbook, like Claire has.

"Hey." Michael gently nudges me. "Where did you go?"

"Nowhere. You thought you were helping me."

"Actually, I was being awkward and didn't know how to flirt with you. I think about you when you aren't here. I run through everything we say... And that's one of the only moments I regret with you."

Michael takes a deep breath, the type of breath where you know something bigger is coming, and I stay quiet. No quippy response, no sarcastic jab, no romantic interjection.

"I don't know what it's like in the future, but I can tell you're a confident guy, Andre Cobb from Boston. You're sure of yourself. You're brave. You stand up for what you think is right. That's admirable. That's something we need more of."

"I don't think I'm that brave. This is the seventies. You don't know it, but a lot of things are going to happen in the next twenty years. A lot of things have already happened now. The peace-and-love movement, civil rights, women's rights. Those people are brave."

He nods. "I agree. But that's collective bravery. It's easier to be someone, to do brave things, when you have people beside you. What you do? That innate strength inside of your heart? That's part of you. Being out and being proud? Being Black and gay? None of that must be easy, no matter what time it is."

"It's easier now than I'm sure it is for you," I counter.

"Maybe, but I'm still white. That helps everything." He grins, but it doesn't reach his eyes like before. This time, the joke is just to clear the air. "I haven't been frank with you, Andre."

My body wants to root itself to the concrete when Michael says that, but I force myself to keep walking. There's a rawness in his voice, a cracking vulnerability, like old paper in the hands of a reckless child. He avoids my eyes as we walk half a block, opting to focus on his booted feet instead.

Right then, in that hairsbreadth of a heartbeat, I realize that this is the make-or-break moment.

"Well, there's no time like the present to be honest, yeah?"

Michael and I stop at the Greenway, or rather, I do. Right here is where one of the greenest areas of Boston should be, the park with the Rings Fountain and sprawling patches of artificial, overly verdant grass.

But there's nothing like that here. Just concrete, streetlights, and cars. We learned about the history of Boston my freshman year—we had to take a whole class on it. But seeing the pictures, and being here now? Those are two different things.

"I never told you what happened when I got kicked out," Michael says, pulling my attention back to him. Again, he avoids my eyes and leans against a wall, his right foot pressed against the brick of an abandoned building. Reaching into his pocket, he fishes out a pack of cigarettes and lights one fluidly.

"You told me it was because you're gay," I remind him.

He shakes his head. "Only partially. My parents found out I'm gay, yes. One of my mom's neighbors saw me coming out of some building with a guy, must have seen me kiss him or something, I don't know. It doesn't matter. Pops called me a faggot. Told me to change or get out.

"But that's not all. I saw my mom in the store a few weeks ago. We were polite—Mom is always polite. I offered to help her with the groceries. She accepted, and we went to her car. She even gave me some money, said, '*Based on how you're looking, you need it.*' When in fact, what I needed was a mother who cared about me."

He sighs, and I can tell he wants to stop. But he also wants—no, *needs*—to keep going.

"I asked her, you know. Why she let him kick me out. Why she didn't fight for me. You know what her answer was? She told me it was because everything about me disgusted her. And if it wasn't who I slept with, then it would be something else. My political views, my profession, the fact that I don't support the war. She was ashamed of everything about me.

"So I left. Stormed out of the parking lot and never looked back."

I reach up and squeeze Michael's shoulder. He doesn't lean into it, but he doesn't tense either.

"I'm sorry, Michael."

"It's not your fault I left."

"No," I say. "But that doesn't mean I'm not sorry that it happened to you."

He shrugs and takes another drag, a shaky one. "Just promise me that it gets better. Promise me that you're not a fluke, that there are many queer guys like us being proud and thriving and, you know…existing."

I don't even have to hesitate this time. "I promise."

"You lying?"

"Does it matter if I am? You might not be alive to know."

Michael shoves me hard, hard enough for me to lose my footing. Once I regain it, I push him back.

"Hey! Who's to say I won't be alive in…fifty-one years? I'll be what, seventy? That's not that old!"

"Keep smoking like that, and you won't be!"

Michael hesitates, looking at the half-smoked cigarette in his hand, and stomps on it twice. "There, now you're stuck with me, even in the future. You're going to regret saving my life fifty years from now, Andre Cobb from Boston."

"Leave that decision up to me, Michael Gray from Boston."

Michael's brow furrows. "Does that really sound as pretentious when I say it as it does when you say it?"

"Oh, absolutely."

"Note to self: stop saying that."

I follow, but deep down, I'm not sure I want him to stop. I like the way my name rolls off his tongue.

Which leads me to some other pretty naughty thoughts that I probably shouldn't be thinking about as he leans in to kiss me again.

EIGHTEEN

This time, the jump back to the McIntyres' home is seamless.

Well, mostly seamless.

There's no stumbling, no shifting from sitting to standing—or from standing to landing on my ass on the floor. There's a sharp pain and a wave of nausea that flies through me, but I guess you can't jump fifty years through time without any sort of side effects.

I check the clock on the mantel—it's been about five minutes since I left. I remember what Claire told me before: one hour in the past is one minute in my time.

And it still didn't feel like enough time.

The dining room is empty now, but there are echoes of life here. I hear someone putting dishes away in the kitchen. Music wafts out from the study. Everyone is in their own separate area of the house, like creatures licking their wounds. I take two steps toward the hallway, intending to slip out, but Blake walks through the foyer and into the dining room.

"Hey," he says curtly.

"Hey back."

Awkward silence. I hate it. I'm never the type of person who can just let it be. I need noise. I need stimulation. I need *something*. So I do what I always do when the silence wants to swallow me whole.

I speak.

"I'm sorry about dinner. I shouldn't have said anything."

"It's…it's cool. Not your fault."

"Okay, I just feel like I made it worse."

"I said it wasn't your fault, Andre. Drop it."

I quirk my brow in response. "I'm just trying to apologize. You don't have to—"

Before I can finish, Blake interjects. "Not everything centers around you, Andre. Despite what my mom might have told you or led you to believe, you're not the center of this family's life. We existed before you, and we'll have the same problems after you're gone."

The curtness and the way Blake's words slice, with the intention of mortally wounding, throw me off-balance. He brushes by me, grabbing the pitcher of iced tea, which still sits on the table, and pours himself a glass, the bicep of his right arm flexing while he does it.

"Did I do something to piss you off?" I ask.

Give him the benefit of the doubt, Andre, I think. *Maybe something happened that you're missing.*

"Nope."

Blake doesn't even look up at me as he sits down, sipping

his drink angrily—if that's even possible. His back is hunched over, almost caveman-like. It's like the only thing keeping him from lashing out is, in fact, the drink in his hand.

"Okay, well, clearly I did so… Let's talk about it."

"I'd rather not."

Still no gaze, no visual cues as to what I might have done. I sigh and sit, waiting. Ten seconds turn to twenty, twenty to forty, but still, Blake stands his ground.

I have to give it to him. Being as stubborn as he is? That's not easy.

"All right," I say. I give up, standing and pushing the chair in. "I'm just going to go. Hope you enjoy your dessert, or whatever, and your parents stop fighting."

I don't make it halfway through the dining room before the loud clatter of utensils rips through the air.

"You just don't get it, do you?"

I turn to face him, arms crossed. I've dealt with people like Blake all my life, especially at school. Entitled kids who think the world revolves around them. Who think everyone in their life should be a mind reader, able to predict every thought they have.

I learned early on how to deal with people like that. I learned how to play the game.

"Well, if I did get it, I'd like to think I'd be able to help. But since you don't think I understand, how about you explain it to me, hmm?"

He wipes his mouth angrily.

"It comes so easily for you, doesn't it? Being successful, succeeding, people liking you." He takes a step forward, his voice low. "You know, some of us actually have to work f—"

"Don't." My voice comes out ice cold. "Don't you dare come and talk to me about how hard your life is."

"Oh, are you going to tell me you have it harder? You're going to compare your life to mine, because you think you know me just because you're in my house?"

"I never said *any* of that!"

"You were about to!"

We're inches apart from each other now. I'm not sure if Blake's parents can hear us arguing, if they're still so deep into their own debate that they don't care, or if they can't hear us at all. The only things I can hear are the blood pumping in my ears and Blake's voice. They mix together like a war drum, each word, every pump egging me on.

"I don't even know what you're so angry about right now!"

"Of course you freakin' don't!" he roars, loudly enough for the room to shake. "You don't know how lucky you are! To have a gift like this! To be chosen by my parents!

"Forty-six. That's how many people were eligible to receive my brother's liver. That means you had a one in forty-six chance of getting it, a two point two percent chance. And you think, what, you were lucky?"

"You're just saying shit now to piss me off," I growl.

He shakes his head and puts some space between us. "You're not that stupid, Andre."

"I got this liver because I was the best candidate on the list, and it was the right liver for me."

"Sure, you're half right. You got it because you were the best candidate. But not for whatever scientific reason your doctor told you."

All I want to do is punch him.

"My parents selected you, Andre. They looked at all the files to decide who would be best to receive my brother's liver. They weighed the pros and cons of who should receive the chance to be gifted with time travel, and they selected you. Who would be the best person to take that chance, who would be the least likely to reject it? You're not special in the way you think you are. You're special because my parents think you're special."

"I don't believe you."

But do I, though? It always felt...too perfect. Even when it happened, the perfect liver, at the right moment, on the right day? Mom and Dad told me that miracles happen, and that we don't question them, which sounded strange to me, considering they're scientists. But even scientists believe in a higher power. I guess miracles are just like that.

"Why?" I ask.

"Why what?"

"Keep being short with me, and I'll leave," I threaten. "I'm not the enemy here."

Blake mutters something under his breath that sounds close to a string of curse words. But, like a restrained dragon, he breathes heavily through his nose and relaxes, the tenseness in his broad shoulders calming.

"Why what?" he repeats, softer this time.

"Why would they select me?"

"I told you before. We're a dying group of people, Andre. Time travel has been in my family for generations—at least six. My mom and dad are from Traveler royalty. When my dad lost his ability to travel... It was just a glitch. It happens with age sometimes. Sometimes you lose it, sometimes it comes back, sometimes it's limited.

"But when I was born unable to do it, and—"

"It means that the time-traveling gene is dying," Claire says from the doorway. Both Blake and I jump. Her face is almost unreadable, like a Mona Lisa of anger, sorrow, frustration, and calculation. The only sign of genuine regret is the slow tapping of her right index finger, like Morse code, on the doorjamb.

"Andre, will you join me in the study? I think we should have a conversation, just you and me. You deserve to know the truth—the whole truth."

NINETEEN

I'm hesitant to follow Claire.

It's not like we haven't been in here before. In fact, the study is the most familiar part of the house. But something about this feels very mob-boss movie to me. How she walks in silently, closes the sliding door behind her. How she sits on the couch and gestures for me to sit across from her. How I obey. It's all very *Godfather*—part one, of course, the best *Godfather*.

But she's smart and knows my weakness. It's the one thing that identifies me as being my parents' son: I love knowledge. I live for it. Having information—all of it—is power. Information isn't harmful or good; it's neutral, and it's about how you use it.

And Claire has all the information I could ever want.

But the silence? That I could do without.

"Ask anything you want," she finally says.

"Is he telling the truth?"

She pauses. "My son, intentionally or not, speaks in half-truths. There is some honesty in what he's saying, of course. But he doesn't know the whole picture."

"Because you didn't tell him, or because he's choosing not to tell me?"

"The former." Those two words don't come out easily. "You have to understand where I...where *we* were coming from."

"I really don't, Mrs. McIntyre," I interject. "I appreciate what you gave me, I really do, but that doesn't matter if it's not the whole story. I don't remember the philosopher who said this, but a good deed doesn't matter if it comes with bad intentions. You gave me this liver because you were experimenting on me."

"I was not," she says. Hurt clouds her face. "I'm not that kind of person."

"I believe you." Or, at the very least, I believe that she doesn't *think* she's that kind of person. But somehow, that truth rings false. Like when someone says they're not racist, but their actions prove differently. "Then why did you do it? Give me the liver?"

"Because you needed it."

"And also because you were hoping, like Blake said, to pass on the time-traveling gene."

"Those two things are not exclusive, nor do they need to be!"

I sigh and stand. I pace, walking back and forth in front of the bookshelves, filled with memories and histories that Claire has probably lived firsthand.

"You're upset."

"I'm not." At least, I don't think I am.

"Then betrayed? Hurt? Abused?"

Do I feel betrayed? No. That's not the word I'm looking for. Neither are the other ones. I don't know this family well enough to feel those things. The emotional hooks of friendliness and found family haven't sunk into my flesh yet. If anything, I feel...validated.

Isobel was right. The lives of the rich are so far removed from our own that it's like we don't exist—or even coexist. We're two parallel existences.

I should just walk out the door, I think. It's my liver. I don't owe them anything. I don't need to be here. Time travel or not; it's my choice.

Instinctively, I put my hand over my organ and feel the faint scar. It healed nicely, barely leaving a bump.

See, Dad had said, examining it. *That's the type of surgeon you can be. You've experienced firsthand how important it is to be good—no, great—at what you do. You'll never forget this, champ. Maybe, if there's one good thing that came out of this cancer, it's showing you how much good you can do as a doctor.*

Now those words make me sick to my stomach, like they're rotten eggs just sitting in the pit of my bowels.

I don't want to be a doctor.

I don't want to be a surgeon.

Right now, I don't know what I want to be. But I do know that I just want to be Andre, and now, for the first time in a year, I feel like I have the chance to decide what and who I want to be. And I'm certainly not going to let this weird family have any say in it.

My phone rings—loudly. The sound makes me and Claire jump. The ring is particular: shrill, loud, and unforgiving.

"That's my VIP ringtone," I mutter, fishing out my phone. It can only be one of three people: Isobel, Dad, or...

"My mom."

I stare at the picture, my mom's angular face, dark brown skin, and Afro on display, her broad face smiling contagiously back at me. She has me pulled in close, though I'm half out of the frame. She loves this picture. It's her contact photo for me too, with her face cropped out and mine in the center.

"I need to take this."

I don't wait for permission because I don't need it. Slipping out and into the kitchen, I take a breath, mentally counting how many rings I have left before it goes to voice mail, and then I pick up.

"Hey, Mom. I—"

"Get home. Now."

What time is it? I pull my phone back to check—only 7:54. And it's summer.

"Is everything cool? I'm just out with—"

"Andre Forrest Cobb, if you are about to lie to me right now about where you are, I swear to God I'm going to..."

She pauses, and my breath hitches. Not out of fear, but because my parents have never had to punish me. Before cancer, I wasn't a liar; I wasn't a problem kid or someone who snuck off. The "Black people need to be ten times as good" talk was given to me early, and it rooted itself, like a watermelon seed in someone's stomach, and grew. Work hard now, play hard later. I embodied that.

This is new for both of us.

"Just get home," she says. "I know you're not at Isobel's. I called her."

"You're checking up on me?"

"Really?" I can hear the eyebrow raise in her voice. "You're the one who lied, and you're going to try to accuse me?"

Her voice is begging me to challenge her if I dare, but I keep my mouth shut.

"Be home in twenty minutes," she orders.

"It takes closer to thirty-five to get home from here."

"Then you better leave now."

And then the line goes dead, leaving me to stew in the vague dread of what will follow when I get home.

TWENTY

According to my parents, a punishment worthy of lying to them is being grounded for two weeks.

"Library and home, that's it," Mom had said the next morning. "You can leave your phone on the kitchen island while you're working. The laptop must be used in the living room. If your father and I aren't home? Then I guess you'll need to get up early the following morning."

The tension in the house is palpable. We don't know how to exist among one another. It's like we're three different planets, in three different orbits, trying to avoid colliding with one another.

Being grounded is an awkward place to be. Mom and Dad try to keep things as usual. And I do my best to remember that this is my own doing.

I lied.

I broke their trust.

I deserve this.

But that doesn't keep the disdain from growing like cancer

deep within me. If they knew the whole story, maybe they'd understand. If they knew I could time travel, if they knew I had used that ability to meet a boy—a really awesome, smart, kind, funny boy—then maybe they'd get it. Because it's not like I'm going to talk to the McIntyres anymore. This is just adding insult to injury.

I'd only risk making my parents angrier for someone like Michael.

But they can't know that.

It's six o'clock in the evening, about eight days after my initial grounding, when there's a knock at the door. Mom, Dad, and I are at the dinner table eating Chipotle, the takeout choice of the night, thanks to both of them working late and coming home not in the best of moods.

Dad looks up first. "You expecting anyone?" he asks, posing the question to both of us but only looking at Mom. Ever since I lied, he's been unable to hold eye contact with me. It's like the break in trust is so great, so profound, that the wound will never heal, and he can't look at me the same.

It's ridiculous. Dramatic. And not nearly as important a concern in my life as it used to be. It's funny how things like being able to time travel will change your priorities.

Mom shakes her head, halfway through a bite of her burrito. But no one moves. The knock repeats itself, this time harder, louder.

"Don't everyone rush at once. I'll get it," I muse, standing up.

Mom mutters something under her breath; I'm sure it's a shot across the bow. She's been doing that ever since the argument. At least I'm smart enough to know that taking the bait will only end badly for me—probably a longer sentence of house arrest.

And, frankly, I'm going stir-crazy.

Clyde trots behind me, like the security guard that he is. The smell of whoever is at the door must be unfamiliar to him, which means it's not Isobel. She's already stopped by once, only to get rebuked at the door by Mom, the gatekeeper preventing entry.

But at this point, any break of my mundane routine interests me, even if it's just some salesman at the door or someone campaigning for the mayor.

At least, that's who I expect.

But when I open the door, that's not who's there.

"Hey," Blake says.

There's no emotion behind it; it's like a cold stone hitting me in the side of the head.

But when Blake says it, in his deep baritone voice, it sends shivers down my spine, and I swear my heart skips a beat, even if just for a fraction of a moment. Blake McIntyre is standing here, in a pair of jogging sweats and a light-colored T-shirt. In front of my house.

"Hey. How did you…"

He arches his brow.

"Of course. Did your mom travel back in time or something?"

He holds up his phone. "Not hard to find where someone lives if you are clever enough. Can we talk?"

I want to reply with some quip, like how *clever* and *Blake McIntyre* aren't two words that I would put together. But that feels like a shot below the belt, and considering that the last conversation we had wasn't…great, I swallow those words down.

"Sure. Move, Clyde."

Clyde nudges his way between my legs, sniffing the air. He stares at Blake, judging him, sizing him up, deciding whether to give him his seal of approval and whether he's worthy of being in my presence.

Blake glances down apprehensively. "Should I be worried?"

"Clyde's a big fluff ball, the definition of all bark and no bite," I promise, patting his head. Clyde sniffs the air, moving half a foot closer to Blake and tentatively licking his leg. "See?"

Slowly, Blake extends his hand to Clyde, who returns the act of trust with another lick.

"I didn't know you had a dog."

"You never asked," I say truthfully.

Blake opens his mouth and then closes it before opening it again, obviously picking other words to say. "That's part of the reason that I'm here, actually," he admits. "Can I come in?"

My pulse quickens again. Even though I'm pissed at my parents, I'm not ashamed of them. Never have been and never will be. I'm not ashamed of anything about my life. But something about having Blake inside of my home? It feels wrong—feels…dirty. And I can't fully explain why.

"I'll be quick, I promise."

"That's not what's..." I sigh. "I'm grounded." I say it like it's some dirty word, something I should be ashamed of admitting. Teens get grounded all the time. Isobel has been grounded at least a dozen times since I've known her. But being a "good kid" was a badge of honor for me. And now it's gone. It's something I'll never get back. Maybe my parents' validation means more to me than I thought.

"Seriously?"

I nod. "Two weeks."

"No friends? What's the name of that girl I saw before?"

"Isobel."

"Yeah, her. She's not here?"

I shake my head. "Only home and the library and back again."

"Well, then that's perfect, since, as we've established, we're not friends."

Before I can let him know that those semantics won't matter to my parents, Blake pushes himself inside, walking quickly in his sneakered feet toward the sound of idle chitchat between my parents.

"Hey! You...wait!"

If there was any time for my pulse to race, now is the time. I close the door quickly behind me and gently tap Clyde's rear, ushering him into the living room. "Stay."

"Blake," I hiss, walking quickly behind him. My heart rate increases with each step. The space between the dining room and the hallway decreases with each second that passes.

I have no idea what's going to happen when Blake and my parents meet, but I know one thing: no good comes from two worlds colliding.

"Mr. and Mrs. Cobb," Blake says in a voice that sounds like silk. "Hi there, I don't know if your son told you about me. I'm in his class at school. Advanced Trig."

"Calculus," I say quickly, correcting him. "Blake was in Trig and switched to Calculus."

"That's right," he says, without missing a beat. "Calculus."

The slipup doesn't faze Mom and Dad; they're both already thrown off-balance thanks to Blake's charm. Who just enters someone's home? Who just barges in unannounced?

A white male, that's who.

But Blake also carries himself with a certain charm, a charm that I guess no one is immune to. I wonder if he's always had it. Does it come naturally to him? Did he have to learn it? Can you even learn charm? It seems like something you're just born with.

"Nice to see that Andre is making good friends," Mom says. That's a dig, but I let it go. "Not that I don't like Andre making friends, but why...?"

"Am I here? Good question," Blake says, turning to me. "I'm surprised you didn't tell them."

This is when I'm supposed to ad-lib and riff off him. I've seen it done dozens of times in TV shows.

"I didn't think I was allowed to have guests over," I say slowly, still parsing through the words. "I'm grounded."

"Well, I think your parents would make an exception for a school project, right?" Blake asks, turning to them. "Am I right, Mr. and Mrs. Cobb? Education is more important than punitive action?"

The air in the room is still, and I can't breathe. I'm ready for them to kick him out right then and there, and for me to be in *more* trouble than I was before.

"A project for an online class?" Mom asks. "An online *math* class?"

Blake glances at me, his eyes saying so much more than his mouth ever could. I sigh. What's one more lie going to hurt?

"Yeah, we talked in the class chat and saw that we were in the same area, so we decided to work together. Blake here isn't that great at math and…"

"And considering that calculus is such an important skill for a doctor, you thought you'd help him?" she finishes for me.

My stomach tightens along with my jaw and I nod. "Yeah. That."

Mom glances at both of us for a moment, searching for any scrap of a lie on our faces. She's good at that, finding something to latch on to and exploiting it, making people cave and give her what she wants. Mom's the type of person most people end up owing favors to.

But, after almost five seconds, she relents.

"I've never heard of a calculus project, but then again, schools are getting more and more competitive every day. Door open, but yes, you can work."

I hear the words leave her mouth, I even feel Blake walking up the stairs and pulling me along to follow, like he knows where my room is, but I can't believe it. Even as my body takes the lead and closes the door behind him, I'm silent. Dumbfounded might be the right word, but I can't form the right word.

Until Blake speaks.

"I know I shouldn't be here, considering that we aren't friends and all. But I wanted to say something, so just hear me out?"

He doesn't give me a chance to respond before he continues speaking. If he had, he'd have heard me say, *Sure*. Blake's not the only one in the wrong here.

"I was wrong."

"Again," I add firmly.

He nods. "Yeah, I was wrong again. To, you know, lash out at you. You were brought into this world without asking for it. It's not your fault that my mom didn't give you all the information. And I know my brother. He'd be happy that someone like you got his liver. He'd be happy that *you* have his liver. He'd like you. Hell, he'd probably be your friend."

I listen intently, picking up on every word. Individually, they make sense, but together? Is Blake McIntyre apologizing?

I could reply with some quippy attack. But instead, I pull it back. No *I told you so* or anything similar. Instead, I opt for something else entirely: common ground.

"I really appreciate that," I say, which is honest. "Your brother would be proud of you too."

Blake laughs a throaty laugh that doesn't sound entirely honest and sits on the edge of my bed. "Don't flatter me, Andre. I don't do well with flattery; I get cocky and brazen."

"I'm serious," I say, sitting next to him. "Think about it. You've taught me, or are teaching me, how to time travel."

"I'm pretty sure you're learning that on your own," he notes. "You're a natural, Andre. I've really only given you, what, one lesson?"

"One and a half."

"See." He nudges me. "I rest my case."

"Hey." I squeeze his shoulder and let my hand linger a moment too long. "Even those one and a half lessons were important. In hindsight, maybe shoving me into the past— literally—wasn't a horrible idea."

Blake's green eyes settle on my hand, then slowly move up to my face. There's something almost innocent in his eyes, like when a parent tells a child they are proud of them.

"Point is," I continue, "I wouldn't be as good as I am without you taking the initiative to push me in the right direction. No pun intended."

"No one has ever said that to me before," he mutters.

"I find that hard to believe."

"No, seriously. It was always Dave who got the praise. Not that I'm complaining. He was better."

"And I find *that* even harder to believe." Finally, I take my hand away, setting it awkwardly in my lap, the warmth of his shoulder burned like a birthmark on my palm. "Well, I didn't know Dave, I only know you, and if I'm being honest, you're pretty awesome, Blake."

No words leave his mouth, only a condescending snort.

"I'm serious. The way your parents treated you was wrong. You were in the right to stand up to them. You're the captain of your lacrosse team. You're smart. I think you're doing pretty well for yourself."

He sighs, pinching his nose, and looks up at the ceiling. His gaze lingers on the ceiling, and I see his mouth silently making words before he pulls his head back.

He's cute when he's thinking, I think. Focused and driven in a way that makes his brows furrow and valleys appear on his forehead. It's adorable, really.

It's comforting to see someone else do something that you do. It makes my shoulders relax; it focuses me. It makes me see him in a more human way. In this moment, he's not Blake, the son of time travelers and one of the wealthiest families in Boston. He's just Blake McIntyre, a teen like me who's stumbling over his words.

Focus, Andre.

Finally, he turns to look at me.

"I want to teach you. Like, actually teach you. I want to give you real lessons as much as I can. I can't travel like Mom can or like Dad used to be able to do, but unlike you, I've been around time travelers my whole life. I've learned from them. I've heard them talk about their mistakes and struggles. I know I can help you, if you still want me to and you're willing to give me a chance."

I hesitate before answering. Not because I don't know what I want to say, but because I know I should think this over. Ever since getting drawn into the McIntyres' lives, things have gotten more complicated, not easier. But I have a duty, to myself, to Blake, and to Dave to master this. To learn how I can really use this.

And if I do it right, I can go back and see Michael whenever I want. That's a win-win to me.

I extend my hand to him to shake. "All right, let's do it. Third time's the charm, right?"

Blake grins a smile that shows his dimples and grabs my hand in his own, shaking it firmly.

"Third time's the charm," he repeats. This time, his hand lingers when I try to pull back, and once he finally lets go, once he finally stands to leave, hugs me goodbye, and I watch his car drive away, I wish I had held on longer.

TWENTY-ONE

"Holy shit."

It's been almost a month since Blake came to my house, and since then, every other day, I find time to go to his. We have a schedule—Mondays, Wednesdays, and Fridays, he picks me up at the library at one, which gives me enough time to work on my classes, so that I won't fall behind, but isn't so late that we can't get some training done. We work till about five or six, and then I head back home. Mom and Dad, so far, haven't been the wiser.

This time, we're practicing traveling farther back than 1969.

This time, I come back soaking wet.

Blake looks up expectantly. He glances at me, arches a brow, and then looks at his watch. "Three minutes this time. Solid. But you're soaked! Where did you—"

"Nineteen twelve," I say through chattering teeth and the pain that is blossoming in my side. The pain after jumping is getting more severe, but I don't want to tell Blake that. He jumps up and gets me a towel from downstairs. It smells like lilacs and honey, and it's warm. Of *course* the McIntyres are one of those fancy families with a towel warmer in the bathroom.

"Nineteen twelve? That's farther than you were supposed to go," he says, rubbing my arms slowly, to keep me warm. "What's it like then?"

"Think about it," I say, as the feeling begins returning to my body.

It takes him a moment, but when he gets it, his arms stop moving.

"Oh. The *Titanic*?"

"Mm-hmm." I pull back. I move to sit on the couch but realize that it's not a good idea in my current state. I can still feel the pins and needles of all that ice-cold water on my body. "I was there when it was going down."

"Did you see Rose and Jack?"

"You know they aren't real people, right?"

He shrugs. "Could have been. Here," he says. "Let me get you some dry clothes."

He disappears before I can tell him no. There's something…personal about wearing Blake's clothes.

But the idea of his skin touching mine via the conduit of his clothes? There's something personal about that too.

Or, maybe, as Isobel would say, I'm overthinking it.

They are just freaking clothes.

Moments later, he returns with a pair of shorts and a T-shirt.

"Bathroom's—"

"Down the hall to the left, I know." For a second, I'm worried that the joke won't land, but he smiles back and hits the side of his head.

"Yeah, you do. You've been here enough times."

Half a minute later, I return, warm and dry, and the pain has lessened to where I almost don't notice it. Usually we take time to debrief—discuss what happened or what went wrong—more often than not, what went wrong. But this time, Blake doesn't do that. At least, not yet. This time, he whistles.

"You know, you look good in my clothes," he says with that cocky sideways grin on his face. "I guess I'm good at picking clothes."

"Oh, shut up."

"Maybe I should be a fashion designer," he muses, tapping his chin. "I could name my brand…"

"Time after Time?"

He shakes his head. "Too on the nose."

"The Time Traveler's Wardrobe?"

"Are you taking that from the movie *The Time Traveler's Wife*?"

"You mean the greatest movie of all time? Yes."

"Whoa." Blake throws his hands up in the air. "That is *not* the greatest movie. False. Mendacity."

"You're going to pull out 'mendacity,' and I bet you don't even know what movie is known for that line."

Blake snorts. "*Cat on a Hot Tin Roof*. Don't play with me, Andre. I know my movies."

I quirk my brow and cross my arms over my chest—maybe even puff it out a little. "Yeah? You do? All right, fine then. Name your top five movies of all time. We'll see how well you know movies. Go."

"Oh, that's easy." Blake doesn't even hesitate. He grabs my wrist and yanks me down the hall and downstairs into the basement, a part of the house I've never been in before. It's got the same cherry wood as the rest of the house. Pillars of stone line the walls along with a dozen leather chairs.

This is an actual movie theater, in the basement of his house.

But what I'm paying attention to the most? The fact that Blake's hand still holds mine as he leads me to the bookcase full of movies.

"*The Wolf of Wall Street, Kill Bill, The Terminator, The Spectacular Now*, and *Alien*," he says with confidence, pointing to the DVD of each one. "I have the Blu-ray and the digital copies too."

I stare at the massive movie collection, where there are easily more than four hundred DVDs. Why does anyone even have this many DVDs?

"Important question," I mutter, still scanning the collection. "*Kill Bill: Volume One* or *Two*?"

"*Volume Two*, obviously."

"Oh, sorry, I have to go now," I say, pretending to pull away and walk up the stairs.

But I can't...not only because I don't want to...but also because his hand is still in mine.

But, really, it's the smile on his lips, the soft, boyish one that is gentle and kind and warm, that makes me stay.

"Do you like *Volume One* more?" he asks, an honest question.

"I do. It sets the tone and has a better story than just endless killing."

He nods, finally letting his hand slip from mine.

"Did I say something wrong?"

Blake shakes his head. "Not at all, I promise." He pauses. "Dave loved the first one too. We would argue about it all the time. He used the same logic too. You're more like him than you think."

"Or is this some transference thing," I say under my breath.

"Sorry?"

I gesture blindly, as if that would help him understand. I'm a hand-talker, after all. "I read about it. Stories of people who get transplants and suddenly have new skills. A woman who gets a kidney and suddenly can play the piano. A guy who gets a lung and can speak Spanish. The body carries with it more than we let on."

"And you're thinking that maybe, because Dave had the same opinion as you about *Kill Bill*, it's him talking and not you?"

I nod. "Could be."

Blake nods too. "Could be. But let me ask you something. Would you have answered that question the same way if we had met six months ago?"

I pause and think before nodding. "Yeah, I think so."

Blake nods, and his eyes turn a shade darker as he retreats into himself. The same weightless fear fills my stomach again. I know Dave is a sensitive subject. Maybe even bringing him up tangentially is too much.

"Then there's your answer." He thinks for a moment. "But I will say this," he says. "I think you are your own person. Not my brother. Not a Frankenstein fusion of him. You're Andre Cobb. And you're a pretty cool guy how you are right now.

"And besides, my brother isn't the type of person to encroach on someone's freedom like that. That doesn't sound like him at all. But, more importantly…" He clears his throat. "If you *were* some Frankenstein fusion of my brother, it would make me asking you out even creepier."

"Oh, I fully agree. That *would* be weird." I chuckle, the weight of the whole conversation off my shoulders.

"Agreed." A beat passes. "So can I take you out sometime?"

TWENTY-TWO

I don't answer Blake. In fact, I make up some excuse and bolt from the house. Then three days later, I get a text.

Hey, you.

                                        Hey yourself.

Hark! He answers! Sound the alarm!
Blow Gabriel's horn!

                                        Don't be glib.

Glib? That's a new one to describe me.

                          Do you even know what it means?

Glib, adjective: fluent and voluble but
insincere and shallow.

Did you look that up right now?

No! I'll have you know, I'm not just a
handsome face with a nice body. I am
decently smart too. You know I'm going
to go to Harvard, right?

Is that supposed to be some major
selling point?

Not major, but still something to consider.
Ah, I see. Good to know.

Thirty minutes later, Blake sends a follow-up.

So...?

So...?

You never answered me.

About what?

Now who's being glib?
About, you know, the date.

Ah, that.

Is that a no?

                                        No, not a no.

So it's a yes?

                                        I mean...sure.

Sure as in you are excited to go, or sure as
in you are begrudgingly agreeing to it?

                                        Does it matter?

Yeah, Andre, it kinda does matter?

                                        Then it's the former.

Are you sure?

                                        Yes, I'm sure.

That doesn't sound convincing at all.

                              What are you looking for, then?

I don't know but something that means
it DOESN'T seem like a chore.

It's not.

Are you sure?

I'm sure.

All right.

All right.

Two days later, I get another message from Blake. And for the first time since we started texting, I get excited when I see his name pop up.

Do you like animals?

Like, to eat?

No, idiot. To see. Like the zoo.

Oh, yeah sure. I do.

Again with the lack of enthusiasm.
Let me ask again: Would you like to
go to the zoo with me?

Sure, that sounds like fun.

I swear to God, I'm going to get

an ounce of excitement out of you.

Saturday good?

Sounds good.

If you could see me right now, I'd be

rolling my eyes.

I roll my eyes at that text and think nothing of it, until the next day, when Blake sends me two photos comparing outfits. The caption:

Which one do you like better?

I hesitate before answering, then double-tap the first one so a heart emoji appears. He replies with a thumbs-up, and in that moment, it all hits me.

I'm actually going on a date with Blake McIntyre.

Quickly, I text the one person I can trust: Isobel.

This is a bad idea.

Okay, please explain to me what is bad

about going on a date with a hot guy?

A hot white guy with far too much money

and power who lives in his own little

world?

I think you're projecting or whatever
onto him.

                                    You haven't met him!

No, I haven't, but he seems fine—
remember, I looked him up online.

                                              And?

And what?

                              What's your analysis?

I told you—he's fine. He seems…dare I
say it…normal? But more importantly,
where is he taking you?

                                          The zoo.

Okay, that's adorable.

                    Don't you start! You're supposed to be
                                      on my side!

And I am!

When most kids are dealing with first
crushes and heartbreaks, you've been
dealing with cancer and your grades. You
didn't get those experiences like the rest
of us did. Now you have a chance and no
excuse. Blake is a nice person to have those
experiences with. And if worse comes to
worse, I'll just punch him in the face.

I don't think you can get into Harvard
with an assault charge.

Worth it—and you know I'm right.

Maybe.

Love you too. Now show me what
you're going to wear.

I groan loudly after rereading the exchange with Blake from
a few days ago, tossing my phone onto the seat next to me on
the small couch in my parents' room. Mom glances at me in
the reflection of the mirror, turning her body in a three-quarter
view, examining the dress she's picked.

"What's up?" she asks, turning back to face herself. She's

been trying to decide what to wear to the gala for hours now. She left work early today, and I can tell that her hair is different; it smells slightly of hair spray—the same type they use in her sister's hair salon on the other side of town.

This fundraiser for the college must be important if she (a) left work early, and (b) went to Aunt Sheryl's place. They haven't talked since last Christmas—the famous Saunders Christmas incident of 2020.

"Isobel trouble?" she asks, sauntering over to her nightstand and pulling out a pair of diamond earrings.

I shake my head.

"Boy trouble?"

I nod but don't give her any more.

But Blake's not my only trouble. It's been over a month, and I can still feel Michael on my lips. It's distant now, like when Clyde's scent on my bed finally disappears, and I can only smell it by burying my face deeply in the fabric. That's what Michael feels like right now.

The logical question that anyone would ask would be: *If you miss him so much, why don't you just go see him, Andre?* He's literally only a hop, skip, and a jump away.

But it's not that simple. It's like when you know you should call someone, but you don't. Or when you know you have an email to read, but you don't open it. Most of the time, that's out of nervousness; you don't want to get any bad news. And I guess, the feeling I have right now is the same, but different all at the same time.

That moment with Michael was amazing. Truly freakin' amazing. And I don't want to ruin it. I'm getting better at jumping, but what if this time I jump too far? What if I jump three months farther, and Michael has moved on, forgotten about me, and met someone new? Or worse, what if I jump three days from our kiss, and Michael has realized that he made a mistake?

Right now, if I stay here, in my year, I can imagine what I want to happen. There's no reality barging in, forcing me to deal with the truth. I can make up my own future, my own happy ending.

And that's worth it.

Clyde doesn't miss the chance to come padding over, put his front paws on the couch, and lick my cheek, bringing me back to reality.

"Boy trouble?" Mom repeats in a leading tone.

"Not like that, Mom."

"Do we need to have—"

"We one hundred percent do not need to have that talk. Dad already gave it to me. And you did too."

"I did?"

"Twice."

"A third time can't hurt."

I swat Clyde away. "Maybe when I actually have a boyfriend."

Mom leaves the room, heading into her closet for a moment, then returns with a pair of heels. She sets them on the chair by her vanity, checking them against the fabric of her dress.

"Should I be worried?"

"Why would you be?"

"That boy. Blake McIntyre, the son of the woman who gave you your liver and the boy who stopped by last week. He's in one of your online classes, right?" She doesn't actually want an answer. "And he's also the boy who you're so concerned with, who's been taking up so much of your mental space."

She pauses, spritzing herself with perfume and putting on her shoes.

"Being close to those who saved you is good, Andre. But I don't want you to feel like you have to be indebted to them. That's not how an organ transplant works."

"I know."

"And you promise me you'll be careful?"

"I promise."

She nods. That's the end of that.

"So you like this boy?"

I pause. The real question isn't if I like Blake; it's if I like Blake more than I like Michael, and I don't know the answer to that question.

"Let me rephrase." Mom stands and gestures for me to help her with the clasp of the necklace that Dad got her for their twentieth anniversary. Tonight must be an important night. "Do you think you might like this boy?"

I stand behind her, weaving and threading my fingers like it's second nature, helping her with the clasp. It's not long before the necklace falls against her skin. It's beautiful but doesn't overpower her. It allows Mom to shine, and I can see, in this moment, why Dad fell for her—and keeps falling for her.

"I don't know yet, but I know I don't dislike him. There are a lot of factors at play." Like Michael.

"That's enough for now." She turns back around, cups my cheek with one hand, and smiles. I can't help but instinctively nuzzle her hand. It's warm and it's safe and—

"Andre!" Dad's voice rings loudly from downstairs, breaking through the wooden barrier of Mom's door. "There's a boy at the door for you!"

TWENTY-THREE

Blake waits downstairs for me for ten minutes while I run into my room to finish dressing. A button-down shirt that plays well off my dark skin, a pair of skinny jeans, a spritz of cologne, and…

"Boots or sneakers?" I ask Clyde. He looks up lazily, flicking his right ear.

"Sneakers it is."

Downstairs, Blake, Mom, and Dad are sitting at the dining table. Blake went all out in a button-down shirt with the sleeves rolled up, a black vest, and nice jeans.

"That's a different outfit than you showed me," I say. Mom clears her throat and Dad glares. "I mean, you look nice."

"You think?" Blake asks. He looks down at his boots—I'm glad that I didn't select mine—and spins around once. "Thanks. I really wasn't sure what to wear on a date—had a crisis of confidence at the last minute and thought I'd change it up. I knew I was going to have to keep up with you."

"Careful there, Dre," Dad says. "This one's a charmer. Guard your—"

"Dad. That's enough. We're going." I push Blake toward the door, intending to get him out of there as quickly as possible. But before we can cross the threshold, Dad grips my arm, squeezing.

"I'll meet you at the car," I tell Blake, who catches on.

Once Blake's gone, Dad opens his mouth, but I cut him off.

"I know what you're going to say. Can we just skip—"

"Nope," he says, handing me my jean jacket from the door. "You know you don't have to do anything you don't want to do."

"Dad."

"Don't feel forced. This is just a boy. To quote *Grey's Anatomy*, which is a god-awful example of hospital procedures—"

"Please don't. I'm begging you."

"He's very dreamy, but he is not the sun."

"All right," I say quickly and hug him. "I'm going. I'll be home by curfew. Goodbye."

I push my way out and get into Blake's car.

"Drive. Quickly."

The zoo is on the other side of town, and since it's Saturday, the streets are busy. It gives Blake and me time to talk, but for the first fifteen minutes, we both sit in silence.

I'm the one who breaks it.

"So, you were serious about the zoo, huh?"

He glances over but never moves his hands from the ten-and-two position. "Yeah. Is that a problem? Thought it might be nice?"

"Or cute?"

He shrugs. "Both work, I guess."

"You guess?"

He shrugs again. "There's a special late-night event. Seeing animals at night—I thought you'd like it. Don't want to be too cocky. That's not something you like in a guy, is it?"

"You'd be surprised what I like in a guy. Want a hint?"

"I'm not against playing video games on easy mode, so yes."

"You're on the right track."

Blake grins, and I can't help but grin back. There's something different about this smile than others, nothing physically different... But this time?

This smile makes it hard for me to breathe.

"What else?" I ask.

He glances over at me.

"What else do you think I like in a guy?" I clarify.

He shrugs, his eyes still looking forward. "A good person, I think."

"You think or you know?" I bite my lip. "Sorry. Thank you."

"You're a person who doesn't take compliments well." He reaches over with his hand, squeezing my thigh. "Should we unpack that?"

My body freezes and tenses up like petrified wood. Blake notices and moves to shift his hand away, but before he can, I put my hand on top of his.

"I thought this was a date, not a therapy session."

Blake lets out his deep laugh, a baritone ripple filling the inside of the car. I like that sound. It's deeper than Michael's voice.

"Touché," he replies, and moves his hand back to the wheel.

A part of me wishes he would put it back.

"Is that what you want to be?" I ask. "A therapist?"

Blake shrugs. The zoo comes into view on a hill in the distance, lights glittering. "Maybe?" he says.

"That doesn't sound confident."

"I'm not sure my father would support that." He laughs. "Do you think a psychologist would bring honor to the McIntyre name?"

In this moment, Michael's words float back into my mind, along with the intention behind them. How we need to decide what type of person we want to be, without worrying about what our parents want. Without worrying about the expectations of the rest of the world. Maybe Blake and I really do have more in common than I thought. The concern that something you want to do doesn't align with what your parents want resonates with me. Michael doesn't have that concern. He's bold, brave, and free-spirited, and he doesn't take no for an answer. I'm envious of that. But, intrinsically, Blake understands me.

I grin at Blake, reach over, and squeeze his leg in return. "I think you'd make a good psychologist. No, a great one."

A bright smile covers Blake's face. A smile that dwarfs the lights from the zoo. It makes his eyes shine a bright green too.

"And you'll make a good…?"

"Doctor," I lie. For now, it's easier, because I don't have an answer to what I want to be yet.

"Doctor." Blake nods, finding a parking space. He turns off

the car, the warm hum turning into a purr as we sit there in silence.

"You ready to have a good night with me, Dr. Andre Cobb?" he asks, twirling his keys between his fingers. "I promise, if you give me a chance, I'll give you the best night you can imagine."

"That sounds like a tall order."

"I appreciate a challenge; you know that," he whispers. "And you're worth making a fool of myself for."

I study his features, every etch on his face, every twitch of his eye, searching for any sort of lie. But there's nothing. Only pure hope and positive intent.

There's nothing dark or sinister about Blake McIntyre.

"All right," I finally say. "But any snacks we get are on me. I can't have you buying everything."

"Who knew Andre Cobb was such a knight in shining armor?"

"Dre," I correct him. "You can call me Dre."

Blake's eyes beam brighter than I would've imagined possible at such a simple offer.

"Dre it is."

We spend over two hours at the zoo, and even with the crowded groups, overactive children, and sleepy animals, it's a fun date. Blake knows more about animals than I would've expected any upper-class teenager to know, and he takes an extreme amount of interest in the lions, the last exhibit we see. He talks about them for almost three minutes straight.

"Sorry," Blake mutters. "I know I ramble when it comes to animals."

"Don't worry," I say, nudging him with my shoulder. He's blushing, looking down at his feet the whole time. "It's cute. Have you considered being a vet? Or a lion psychologist?"

He looks up, with a puzzled look on his face that's oddly adorable. He opens his mouth like he's going to reply, but then he smiles. "Wait, that's not a real thing, is it? Because it sounds like a freakin' sweet—oh. You're joking, aren't you?"

"And what gave that away, hmm?"

He opens his mouth to say a quippy retort but winces, looking up. One raindrop turns into two, two into four, and like a stampede, everyone in the zoo goes running back to their cars. Luckily enough for us, the lion exhibit is close to the exit, and we make it before getting completely soaked.

"Here," Blake says, reaching into the back and pulling out a towel. "Not sure how clean it is. It's my post-practice towel, but…"

"I'll take it." I rub myself down quickly, ignoring the smell of sweat and cologne that lingers on the fabric. And, if I'm honest, it doesn't smell horrible. It smells like him, and that's not the worst smell.

I pass the towel to Blake, who dries himself in silence. Slowly, he strips off his shirt, revealing his chiseled abs and defined pecs—my breath hitches, again. Blake doesn't seem to notice, and if he does, he's doing a good job of playing it cool. He puts his shirt and jacket back on without a word. As an athlete, I'm sure he's used to being shirtless around guys. This is nothing to him.

It's everything to me. Sure, it's not the first time I've seen Blake McIntyre shirtless, but this time, it feels different. This time, we're on a date.

We sit in silence, listening to the heavy droplets of rainfall on the car windshield. Blake turns the heat on low, and the hissing and hum of the crackling heater are soothing.

"I don't expect us, you know, to just start dating," he says suddenly, breaking the silence. "But I had a good time with you today."

I don't need to hesitate with my answer. "I did too."

"And I'm just assuming, you know, correct me if I'm wrong, that since we both had a good time, we could maybe try to see if we can have another good time, and another, and if we do, maybe we can see what happens?"

"Like in geometry, how it takes three points to verify a line?"

He pauses and shakes his head. "You're such a dork, but, like you said before, I'm growing to love it." Blake shifts the car into reverse. "I should get you home. Don't want your dad to hate me right off the bat."

"Oh, he already does. Don't take it personally."

The joy seeps from Blake's face like ink rushing out of a broken container.

"Joking." I smile. "If you're going to hang with me, you have to get used to these jokes."

"Maybe you should make funnier jokes," he scoffs and starts to back the car out, curling his spine around and putting his hand on the back of my seat. At least, that's where his hand should be.

Instead, it slips around my back and grips my right shoulder. He has a sly smile on his face the whole time, a smile he's trying to hide by making his features twist into something normal.

"You're not slick, Blake McIntyre," I say as his hand slips down and settles on my thigh.

"I'm a little slick. You have to admit it."

I roll my eyes and turn on the radio, looking out the window. But, somewhere between ten and fifteen minutes into the silence after we leave the zoo, my hand slips down, and my fingers lace with his.

TWENTY-FOUR

There's something peaceful about holding Blake's hand, stroking his knuckles with my fingers, and riding in silence as we listen to the radio.

By the time we arrive at my house, it's 10:50 p.m., giving us ten minutes to spare before my curfew.

"Do you want to stay?" he asks, half a minute or so after we've stopped, as the engine cools. "I mean, you can go if you want. I'll see you at my place for your training, but…"

"Nah," I reply, squeezing his hand. "I'll stay."

"Because, you know, you don't have to if you don't want to."

"I want to."

The lights are on upstairs in my parents' room, which faces the street. Mom's car is still gone. I'm sure Isobel has been blowing up my phone, but she can wait.

Right now, and it sounds so cheesy that it makes me sick, there's only Blake and me. And that feels like how it should be.

"You don't find this weird?" I suddenly ask, still resting my head against the window.

"Should I?"

"I mean, I have your brother's liver. That... Doesn't that make us, in some weird way, related?"

I can tell he's thinking, letting the words roll over him.

"I don't think so. I think, as my dad says, it makes you part of the family, but not exactly family. You aren't Dave... And I miss him." Blake pauses and closes his eyes.

"The zoo was his favorite place. Always was. Every birthday we would go there, even when he was in college. He still wanted to visit the zoo. So when I thought about where to take you, the zoo just came to mind first." He opens his eyes and glances sideways at me.

"I think...I didn't take enough of my brother's advice. Who does, really? We think we have so much time with the people we care for. But I admired him, you know? He had a lot of good ideas, and despite how easily things came to him, he never took that for granted. Dave was a good person, the best version of Mom and Dad. I...never told him, but I wanted to be like him. Not because he got Mom and Dad's love or anything, but because he was the type of person you look up to. The one person you want to emulate.

"And I miss him," he says, almost a whisper. "I really freakin' miss him."

I don't think I've ever seen Blake show as much emotion as he does in that one simple sentence. I don't think, deep down, that I thought he had...that much depth. But looking at him, seeing him actually try to fight tears as his eyes turn glossy? It softens any previous thoughts I had about him.

Blake, deep down, is suffering like anyone who has lost of a loved one would. No matter how strong a facade he puts up.

"Does that weird you out? That I took you on a date to a place my brother loved, and you have his liver, and I just spilled my guts to you like that?" He laughs, trying to lighten the moment.

It probably should. I think for any sane, average person it would. But I'm not sure that I, Andre Cobb from Boston, Massachusetts, can call myself sane or normal anymore.

"I think if he were here, he would have told you that it was a great date idea. And I would agree with him."

Blake grins and squeezes my hand again. "So what that means, I don't know. It's unprecedented, sure, but that doesn't mean that we shouldn't take advantage of what we've been given?"

"And what have we been given?" I ask, pushing off the window, looking at him.

I don't expect an answer—or maybe I do. Maybe I hope Blake will put this all together for me. The time travel. Him. The secrets. Michael. His parents. His mother's "experiments." My life is almost entirely different than it was six months ago. That should be a good thing. Change is good, in science, in life, in everything. I should be comfortable with the unknown. That, according to my parents, is where the best things happen.

But right now, I just want someone to tell me what direction to take. What path to walk, which road to venture down.

"I'd like to think we've been given a chance," he says, his voice barely above a whisper, like he's not sure he believes it himself. "A chance to see what this is between us."

"You think there's something?"

"Don't you?"

Do I? This night was great; there's no denying it. But every time I think back on it, on every spark of joy Blake gives me, I wonder, would that spark be a roaring flame if I were with Michael?

"Are you out?" I ask. It's a sharp left turn in the conversation but also a worthy distraction.

He shakes his head. "I'm just not super out, you know? The right people know, and I let people know when I want them to know."

"Are your parents cool with it? I'd imagine having a gay kid when you're members of Boston's high society could be..."

"My dad and I don't talk about that," he says quickly. "My mom and I do, but it's like clockwork. The same three questions all the time: Am I being safe, am I having sex, is this just a phase?" He chuckles, but I can tell it's a forced laugh, to keep the space from being too quiet. To keep him from really confronting how much that hurts him. "They mean well, but... Well, you've met my parents."

I squeeze his hand this time. "Listen..."

"We absolutely don't need to talk about it, Dre," he says gently but with a firm edge to it, making it clear where he stands on the topic. "I'm fine with it, really. College is soon. I'll flourish there. It gets better and all that."

The clock reaches 10:55, and I see the shadow of Dad moving in the window. I sigh, giving his hand another squeeze.

"Bonus. At least you got me home on time. My dad's going to love you for that. I swear, sometimes I think he wishes he had a daughter."

Blake laughs and leans across my body as he looks out my window at my house. I can smell the faint scent of his cologne.

He smells the best in this moment, the way the air smells right after a thunderstorm, while Michael smells of faint cologne and a light musk that comes from too many days focused on one thing and forgetting everything else. Blake is different from Michael, in so many ways, but not a bad type of different.

Finally, he pulls back, but only enough so that our faces are close together.

"Can I kiss you?" he whispers.

I hesitate for a second, which turns into two, and then into five, and then ten. Far longer than anyone should pause when asked by a hot guy, whose voice is nothing more than a low, hungry whisper. But it's not for the reason he thinks.

It's because the memory of Michael's lips against my own feels as real as if it's happening right here. Every smell, every touch, every thought that was going through my head with him in 1970 feels as real as if it were happening right now.

Except it's not. I'm not with Michael.

I'm with Blake, and by the time I can process this, he has already pulled back, clearing his throat.

"I'm sorry," I say, clearing my throat too. "It's not…"

Blake waves me off. "It's fine, really."

"I don't want you to think I'm not…" I pause, thinking over the right word. "Not interested?"

"Is that a question or a statement?"

"Statement."

Blake adjusts his jacket, fiddling with the collar before folding it and opening his door. He signals for me to wait, walks around the car, and opens my door for me. It's a simple gesture, but it makes the inside of my chest turn warm and my cheeks burn.

"Then what is it?"

My mouth suddenly grows dry. Blake deserves to know the truth, doesn't he? Of course he does. Everyone deserves the truth. How did I feel when Claire lied to me? Blake doesn't deserve that. No one does.

So I take a deep breath and explain.

"There's someone else," I say, speaking quickly enough that he doesn't have time to interrupt me. "In nineteen seventy. Michael, I've told you about him. He's the one I'm tethered to."

"Uh-huh…"

"And…I don't know," I mutter. "I just… We've been talking a lot. He's a musician, and he challenges me. He helped me understand that maybe I don't want to be a doctor, and that's huge, you know? And—"

"And you like him." Blake cuts me off before I have to say it. "Except it's a total fantasy, because you guys could never really be together."

"That's not fair," I say slowly.

"Not fair? You're the one who's not being fair." Blake lets out a hurried breath and steps back, pacing. "You know what the funny thing is?" he asks, his voice getting louder. "I thought we were connecting. I thought *I* challenged you. But actually, I was just training you to get to him faster."

Our block isn't the quietest block on this street. It's firmly middle class, and there are always people outside, late arrivals, music playing when there shouldn't be—but arguing in the street this late at night will attract attention.

There's more distance between us now, physically and metaphorically, than ever before. Blake stands several feet away, clenching and unclenching his hands.

"I was going to kiss you tonight. I was going to kiss you so good that you would forget about time travel, about college, about everything.

"But now I see that it wouldn't be good enough for you to forget him," he says, moving past me and walking around to the other side of the car. I stand there, listening to the sharp sounds of the door opening and slamming shut. He rolls his window down, looking at me with hurt, dark eyes.

"I'll see you at my house for training."

"You still want to train me after this?"

"Unlike you, I can separate my feelings and do the right thing. You need a trainer. We work well together. I'm going to keep doing it. If you have a problem with that, talk to my mom."

Blake doesn't pull away immediately. He sits there, his hand on the console, staring at me. "You know you can't be with him, right?" he asks. "He's in the past, fifty-one years in the past. There's no future there."

"I know," I whisper.

"And you know there's a future with me, right? I'm right here, Dre."

Logically, I know that. Deep down, I know that. The safe answer—and the easy answer—is Blake.

So why can't I say so?

He shakes his head, pulls back, and starts the car. "You know what, never mind. Good night."

I step back just in time as he peels off, driving rapidly away. My body feels heavy, rooted in place, forcing me to watch as his taillights disappear and the street falls silent, the only sound the thumping in my head.

By the time I step into the house, he's halfway down the street, and Dad's halfway finished with his first question.

"Absolutely not," I reply.

"But—"

"No."

"Andre, I'm your father."

"Right, and not my PO," I remind him, heading up the stairs two at a time. "I'm not talking about my date with my dad."

"So, it was a date!"

"You knew that!"

"Right, but him thinking it's a date and you thinking it's a date are two very different things."

Standing at the top of the steps, I scoff at him, audibly. "I'm going to call Isobel."

"Oh, so you want to talk—"

"Yes, I do," I say, closing the door and leaning against it, like putting my weight on it will keep him out if he decides to enter.

But Isobel isn't the person I want to talk to.

"Michael," I whisper.

I look down at my hands, the front sides and the back. There's nothing different about them. No blurring at the corner of my eyes, just a vibration that makes me feel like I'm a living, breathing tuning fork.

It doesn't scare me. If anything, it's welcome. The faint sound of the CNN report Dad's watching downstairs blends with sounds of the 1970s and echoes in my ears. It feels like I'm walking from one room to the next but stopping at the doorway, waiting to decide if I'm going to make the jump.

And though there's no fear, there's pain. Sharp, warm, hot pain in the center of my gut.

"Shit," I hiss, doubling over and falling to the floor on my knees. When they make contact, it's like a ripple is sent out. The room morphs, shifting in phases between my room and what looks like a party in a house that's not my own. They flicker back and forth—2021, 1970, 1969—like I can see Michael's timeline washing over me in blurred images. The pain continues to grow, spooling out and taking over my whole body.

Focus, I tell myself. Focus on this room. Focus on Michael. Focus only on that. Push through the pain.

Seconds feel like hours before the pain, like a rubber band, snaps back and disappears. When I open my eyes, though, I'm no longer in my bedroom; I'm in Michael's. He's in bed, shirtless, sitting up, his hair a mess.

"Nineteen seventy," he says, without me asking. "Only a few months later than the last time you were here."

I nod, saying nothing, and pull the covers back, sliding into bed. I turn my back to him and hug a pillow, focusing on the cracked etchings on the wall, wondering what shape I can make out of them. Neither of us speak, but I feel him shift, spoon against me, and wrap his arms around me tightly.

And right now, that's enough.

PART THREE

TWENTY-FIVE

"You've been quiet."

Michael and I have been lying in his bed for almost a day and a half now. Well, that's not quite true. I've been in bed for almost a day and a half. Michael went to get us food and played a three-hour gig on the other side of town that he said he couldn't ignore. But besides that, we've been in bed.

And I've been thinking.

This has become our safe space. Away from the rest of the world, away from the future. Away from Blake. Just me and Michael. No one else. It's a soothing feeling. One of the best. But right now, that feeling is distant, and I barely notice his touch. I thought I had been good at hiding it.

"Hmm?" I ask, looking up. "Sorry, mind's somewhere else."

"I can tell," he muses. A record of the Beatles plays in the background. He's humming along to it softly, with perfect pitch, of course. "Everything okay?"

"Yes," I say, far too quickly. It's not even convincing to me. "No. I don't know. Maybe."

Slowly, he sits up. He's shirtless and only wearing a pair of boxers. His short hair is messy, and there's an aura of sleepiness surrounding him.

"Well, wanna talk about it?" he asks, reaching out and grabbing his cigarettes, lighter, and ashtray. I've given up on trying to stop him from smoking. But at the very least, he moves over to the other side of the bed. I've already jumped back once and had Mom accuse me of smoking, thanks to the scent. It seems even nicotine can travel through time and space.

How do I explain to him what I'm thinking? On the one hand, it's not like he hasn't heard off-the-wall things. He's still around me—a time traveler—so he has to know that nothing about me is normal and that there are plenty of situations where the logical explanation goes out the window when I'm involved.

But what I've been thinking? What I've *really* been thinking? It's risky. It's bold. It's terrifying.

He lights his cigarette, resting the ashtray on his abs. As usual, he offers it to me to take a drag of. I refuse.

"Figures," he teases. "You had to have some flaw."

"Not smoking is a flaw?"

"Not being cool is a flaw," he says, though his voice is heavy with jest. "But back to your problem. You going to spill? I think I've proven that I'm a pretty good listener."

"That you have."

I pull myself up to a sitting position, my back against the warped wall of his apartment. It's not a great hovel, but it's his own, and Michael's proud of it. Gone is the house we both shared through time and space. Now, we're in a place where the water is constantly cold, it's drafty, and the stairs creak so badly that whenever we take them, I swear I'm going to fall through the five-floor walk-up.

"There's a boy, back in my time."

"Oh? Is he good-looking?"

I jab his arm hard but don't answer. Because, yes, yes, he is hot. But Michael doesn't need to know that.

"His brother is the one who gave me, you know." I tap my liver gently—it still hurts from the jump.

"The dead boy? That must be awkward. Being friends with the brother of the guy who gave you his liver."

I nod, and the words I've been thinking come out like a whisper. "But that's not what I'm thinking about. Well, it is, but..."

I sigh, running my fingers through my hair in frustration. I feel Michael grip my shoulder and give me just one soft squeeze to remind me that he's here.

"I broke his heart," I mutter. "Or, at least, I hurt him. How doesn't matter..." I don't have the courage to tell Michael how anyway.

"I'm sure you didn't mean to," Michael reassures me, stroking my arm with two fingers. His light touches feel like electricity on my body, shocking me back to life. "You're a good person, you know? I don't say that about many people."

"I wasn't a good person. I was...selfish." I sigh. "I'm not sure who I am anymore."

Michael's hand keeps moving, but he doesn't speak. It's an old psychology trick—giving the other person space and letting the silence become deafening until they feel like they have to speak.

It works.

"I'm lying to my parents about how I'm spending my time. I'm ignoring my best friend. And don't even get me started on school. I used to be someone who *cared* about things. Someone who had goals and priorities and was more than just…"

The words evaporate before I can speak them, and maybe that's a good thing. Because there's no answer I can think of that doesn't come back to blaming Michael, directly or indirectly. And this isn't his fault. It isn't his fault that I'm here. It isn't his fault that I gained the ability to time travel. He's unlucky, that's all. And he doesn't deserve the brunt of my existential crisis.

"But I can fix it. I can make it all better," I say. "This all started when Dave, the guy who gave me his organ, died. I can stop that from happening."

This time, Michael's hand stops. He freezes like a statue, his cigarette about two inches from his face. Slowly, he turns to face me, his features twisting into confusion and mild apprehension.

"What are you talking about, Dre?"

I've never said it out loud, this plan. It's been brewing in the back of my mind.

But once I start talking, I can't stop.

"I'm a time traveler. I can use that. I know when and where

he died; it's public record. I can…go back and stop this boy's brother—this boy I care about—I can stop his brother from dying. It wouldn't be hard. I can just…I don't know, just stop the car from T-boning him. Hold him up for a few minutes, or, if worse comes to worse, tell him what I intend to do. He'll understand; he's a time traveler. It's not like he won't believe me."

"And what about you?" Michael asks.

"What about me?"

He sighs, putting the ashtray on the table by his bed, the cigarette stomped out in the glass. "You need that liver, don't you? Not just to time travel, but to *live*, right? If he doesn't die, then you don't get the liver. If you don't get the liver, you're back in the hospital."

"I'll convince him to give it to me. Part of it, anyway; the liver regenerates."

Michael arches his brow. "You expect him to do that for you? You're not going to remember him, right? That's how time travel works, all of this—you'll forget him because it never happened, because you didn't get the liver to be able to do these things."

He's beating around the bush, but I know where he's going. He's worried that I'm going to forget him as well. And I will. And maybe he'll forget me too.

"I've thought about that too."

"And? You've realized that this is a stupid idea and can never work?"

"No, I've realized that, if what everyone in his family says about Dave is true, he's a good person. He'll give me part of his liver, and my life can become a little more normal again. His family's life could become normal again."

"How?" Michael pushes back. "You're a smart guy, Dre, but really? This is stupid. It's a half-cocked plan, it doesn't make any sense, and it hinges on the most unreliable of factors: people."

"I have to do something," I argue.

"You are doing something! You're here, you're learning how to time travel. It's not like you're wasting away and drinking his liver to death."

"No," I say, shaking my head. "I have to do something to help him. To *fix* this."

"Why?!" It's the first time I've ever heard Michael yell, and it makes me jump. His voice drips with urgency, and his body is shaking slightly with desperation. "Why do you have to do anything? Why do you have to try to save someone who…?"

And then he stops, his face shifting from anguish to smoothness, like everything has clicked into place.

"It's not just about him," he says under his breath.

"What?"

"This Dave guy, it's not only about him. It's not only about righting some cosmic wrong. It's about…what's his name? His brother's name?"

"Blake?"

"Yeah, Blake. Are you doing this for him? Is he putting you up to this?"

"What?" I shake my head. "No, absolutely not. Blake's not like that."

"Is he forcing you to do this?"

"No, Michael. Again, you don't know him, but he would *never* ask me to do this. He understands time travel; he knows how dangerous it is. He'd probably punch me for doing this."

"Then I really don't understand," he says, looking away from me, like he'll find the answer in the twisted pattern of fabric and blankets.

His gaze moves up, settling on my eyes. Deep within his face, etched like it's been there since the dawn of time, is something that makes my stomach churn.

Hurt.

"You like him. And, clearly, it's more than you like me, because you're willing to risk us never knowing each other to help him," he says.

"Oh my God, Michael, you're…"

"Stop. I think that's why you're really doing this. Maybe you don't realize it yet, maybe you think it's because you're doing it out of the goodness of your heart, but all of that comes back to one thing. You want to make him feel better, to fix him and his family."

Something hot and heavy burns inside of me.

"Michael, I get it. This is a big risk. But my life has totally flipped around. I love that I get to be with you… But I don't know if this is the life I want, especially when it came at the cost of someone else's life. I can't explain it, but I know you're wrong when you say I care more about Blake than I do about you."

"Am I?" Michael asks. "Look at me right now and tell me that you're not doing this only because of him. Because he misses his brother. Because you have the power to make him feel better."

"That's part of it!" I yell, turning to him. "That's what a good person does, Michael! They try to *fix* people. They try to help!"

"There you go again, with your whole 'try to help' and 'be a saint' bullshit! Before, you mentioned everyone you love. Your parents, your best friend…Blake. But you didn't mention me. Or what this is going to do to me. And maybe I'm wrong—God, I freakin' hope I'm wrong. Maybe you don't love him the way I think you do. But if you do this, you're making a choice."

"Wait," I say. "Slow down. What are you saying right now?"

"I think I'm being pretty clear."

"No, what are you trying to say about us?"

Michael pauses again, and this time, it's not to think. He pauses like a breath that's being held or a moment that's being skipped, as if he's trying to decide whether what he wants to say is truly what he wants to say.

"I'm saying that I would do *anything* for you, really. I'd wait for you. I'd live a life where we only have these fleeting moments together. For me, this is enough. But it's not enough for you. I can tell. I—"

"Please, Michael, stop," I whisper as I get up. "I'm going. Because… Well, because of how I feel about you. I don't want the last memory that I have of you to be of this."

December 22, 2020. That's the date I have in my mind. I

know the location, too: the coffee shop where Isobel and I often go for late-night study sessions. A lot of high school and college students go there. And I know that when I leave, my heart will break. But unlike Michael, this isn't enough for me. I love him, but we don't make sense. I can't live half a life. I thought maybe I could, but this last day with him has proven that I'd get lost here with him. Lost in the past, when I should be moving toward my future. And if I don't leave now, I'll never want to leave. I hope he understands.

Warmth pools around my body and mixes with cold. The corners of my eyes start to water, and images blur.

"Andre, I'm serious! Do not leave! If you leave now…"

Rule number two of time travel may be to only jump from point A to point B, but rules are meant to be broken. And that's exactly what I'm going to do.

Whether Michael or Blake or anyone else likes it or not.

———————

———————

There's something unsettling about being in the place where someone died.

I've been around death before. In the hospital one time, about five years ago, when we were visiting my cousin, another kid in the room coded. Mom and Dad did their best to distract me, thinking that, at twelve years old, I was too young to face death. Now, five years later, I'm more familiar with it—and the concept of it—than most teens have to be.

Maybe that's what I should write my college essay on.

But this is different. I have the power to stop this.

And in a few minutes...seven, to be exact...Dave is going to get in his car, head home, and get T-boned by a drunk driver, dying instantly. At least, I like to think it's instant. No one should have to suffer.

I take a moment to massage my side. The pain is intense, but the adrenaline running through me is enough to quell it. After I give myself a few seconds to take a deep breath, I walk half a block, until I'm standing in front of the coffee shop: Jameson's. It's one part bookstore, one part indie music house, and one part piss-poor coffee. A lot of the college students in town come here, and it's a melting pot. As such, the owner caters to that crowd with movie nights, debate nights, and poetry nights. Hell, political watch parties happen here every two years, with ticket sales on a first-come, first-served basis. It makes sense that Dave is here.

I hesitate for a moment before walking quickly toward the door. My mind reels with dozens of scenarios and possible solutions. What if someone I know sees me? What if he isn't here? What if I'm too early? Too late? What if I get distracted?

The possibilities are endless, but only one solution matters: success. I'm not lucky enough to have the luxury of failure as an option. I made a promise to myself. This is the right thing to do. This is what I should do. Fix Dave, and then he'll fix me. Everyone wins.

Except Michael.

Will his life be better or worse without me? I'm not foolish enough to think that my influence on the world is going to have widespread positive, or negative, ramifications.

But affecting one person? Changing one life? That I can do. That I will do. After all, isn't that what everyone, deep down, hopes for? To make a difference in one person's life.

Michael was that person. And the question is, will any of it matter? Even if we do everything right, if my plan goes perfectly...will we still end up together? Part of me desperately hopes so. But I know we don't make sense. I know he shouldn't have to wait for me. He should live his own life.

I can't dwell on the pain of that. Right now, I need to focus. I'm only going to get one shot at this.

Keeping close to a wall, about twenty feet away, I wait. It's not long now—three, maybe four minutes until he leaves. I need to account for him getting in his car, starting it, driving into the intersection. All of that will happen quickly. I need to be ready to act.

What if it doesn't go according to plan? What if something different happens? He's on his way home, doesn't get hit by the drunk driver, but skids into a river instead? Or has a heart attack? Or something else?

The door to Jameson's opens, and deep laughter flows out. A gaggle of half a dozen students, wearing jackets with a mix of different college logos, spills into the parking lot. But I only care about one in particular: the well-built man who looks like a football linebacker, with the jaw of someone who could definitely run for president. The one with the same red hair I saw in the picture, the same red hair his mom has.

The man I've been waiting for.

The feeling of coldness melts away and is replaced with a low, burning warmth. Adrenaline, that's what this is. The rapid heartbeat in my chest, the warm tingling in my fingers, the ringing in my ears, and the way everything feels distant but present all at the same time.

One shot.

One chance.

One moment.

One step. Then another, and another.

I haven't thought through what I'm going to say. Maybe I should have—maybe it all should have been rehearsed, so I could function on autopilot. But I'm best when I'm going off the cuff; I know that about myself. And if I succeed, I won't have much time to think about it and critique myself. Once the clock passes 3:15, and Dave *isn't* dead, everything will change. The world will shift, and this reality won't exist anymore. It doesn't matter how I make that happen, as long as I make it happen.

Simple.

But the sound of a car coming up behind me, closer than it should, and stopping abruptly, jolts me from my thoughts.

And the person who steps out of it makes me forget everything.

TWENTY-SIX

Mrs. McIntyre slams the door of her bright red Prius hard. She's wearing one of those Russian-style faux-fur hats that you see in old movies with a matching infinity scarf. The blacks and reds of her outfit play well off her lipstick and the slight rosiness of her cheeks.

"Are you going to stand out here and get frostbite, or are you going to get in the car?"

Claire and I stand in a silent stare down. What is she doing here? How did she find me?

"Let's go, Andre. That isn't a request," she says softly, subtext heavy in her voice. She's not demanding; she's asking, pleading. This isn't the same Claire McIntyre I've known.

And that scares me.

I study her eyes and look over in the general direction that I saw Dave and his friends walk. I have less than two minutes left. Two minutes to stop him from getting in that car. Two minutes to—

"I'm sure you have a lot of questions about why I'm here," she says.

"Along with other things, yes, that would be a fair statement."

"As do I. I'll explain everything to you, but you have got to get in the car," she urges. "Andre, if he sees you—let alone me? Do you know what that would do to time? I'm risking a great deal to save you from your own mistake."

"I made a choice, a promise," I insist. "I can't just—"

"To Blake? Did he put you up to this?"

"To myself."

"Those are the best promises, but they can be easily broken when logic comes into play. I, for all intents and purposes, am logic." She gestures to her car again, this time with a flourish of her hand. "Please," she whispers.

"If I don't, what are you going to do?" I ask. "If I go and stop Dave…"

"Two things could happen: one, you succeed and change history in a way that cannot be fixed, which violates—"

"Rule number three."

"Or two, the more likely outcome, I'll go back in time and stop you from stopping him."

"And you know I'll do the same."

She smiles, the type of grin where only a corner of her mouth lifts.

"Then we'll just keep going back and forth until one of us slips up and creates a paradox that has bigger ramifications than either of us can resolve," she concedes. "And I surely don't want that. And something tells me you don't want that either, Andre.

And that you're smart enough to know that there really is no other choice for you here."

One minute left.

"Fine," I concede. I circle around her car and slip into the passenger's seat, closing the door behind me. The warmth of the leather seat sends a shiver up my spine, and the blast of dry, hot air relaxes my joints.

Claire follows, and before she even has time to put her seat belt on, I speak.

"What are you doing here?"

She pulls off her gloves, finger by finger, until the thirty remaining seconds pass. We watch as Dave's car peels out of the parking lot and he drives toward us. My breath hitches as he passes us, bobbing his head to some music, tapping his fingers against the steering wheel. He looks…happy. Like that meeting, whatever it was, replenished some well that he had been yearning to fill.

And he has no idea what's about to happen. No idea that in a mile he's going to die. Just like that.

"You and I aren't that different, Andre," she finally whispers, forcing the words out. "We both want to do the right thing. We're both type A people. We both do what we believe is best, consequences be damned." She turns to me, and her eyes are slightly red. Tears glisten at the edges of her eyes. But they don't fall. "The difference is, I've learned with age that some things cannot be changed. Some things have to happen. And this is one of them. Blake really didn't put you up to this?"

"No. I promise. I think, if I'd told him, he would've been against this as adamantly as you are. He isn't as dense or contrarian as you think he is. I'm doing this because I think it's the right thing to do. I don't think Dave should die. And I don't think this is the life I was supposed to lead. I'm doing this for a lot of reasons, but they are all my own. And, honestly, I can't understand why you wouldn't do this. How are you okay with letting your son die?" I blurt it out before I can stop it. "You're a time traveler. You can stop things like this. Fuck the rules."

I know I've spoken out of turn by the way she pauses and closes her eyes. I can *hear* her counting to ten in her head, even if I can't actually hear it. Mom does the same thing when she's angry and holding it back.

"No, Andre. I can't," she finally says when she opens her eyes.

"You can't or you won't?"

"I'm here because I come here every day," she says, her voice breaking just slightly. "I come here to watch my son's last moments. To see him happy. To know that instead of coming straight home from the store, where I'd sent him to pick up eggs, he swung by Jameson's to get a quick drink with friends. To know that I called him, yelled at him, and guilted him into coming home, and because I did, because he peeled out of the parking lot at that exact second to get home to me, he died."

She takes a breath, covering her mouth with her hand. I hear her whimper and choke it back. I feel the tightness in my chest winding.

"But I can't change it, Andre. That's one thing I cannot do. You're right, fuck the rules. I can't change it because that's my code of conduct. Because those are the lines I live by and will not cross. Because if we do not have lines, Andre, with all this power that we have, what will we become? We cannot, even with this power, choose to change things just because *we* don't want to feel pain."

"But why *can't* we?" I argue. "There is a line between abusing power and using it to make the world better, Mrs. McIntyre. You're smart enough to know when not to cross that line."

She chuckles, but it's one of those chuckles that is filled with sadness instead of comedy.

"Stronger men and women than me have thought that they could do exactly what you're suggesting, Andre. And every time, they realize that they have done more harm than good. And it breaks them."

She turns in her seat to face me and touches my shoulder, forcing me to look at her.

"It will break you too. You will make one change and find two other things that you need to change. You'll change those two, and then find four more. You'll never be happy. You'll never create the world you want, and before long, the world you now reside in will become so different, so horrific, that you will do anything in your power to end it.

"But, more importantly, just because we have won the genetic lottery, doesn't mean that we get to be immune from heartbreak. That's what makes us human, Andre. And when you have a power that exists outside the law, feeling human is the only way you remind yourself that you *are* human."

Another group of college students comes out of Jameson's. Police cars speed by. The group looks up, but they continue on with their conversation, heading to their cars.

She sighs, leaning back in her seat for the first time. "Did you consider what would happen to you if you went through with this? To your liver?"

"I'm willing to take that chance."

"You may be, but what about everyone else? The eight billion other people in the world? Even assuming that David's death didn't have bigger ramifications on the global stage," she reminds me gently but firmly. "You can't just assume that you can change one thing and that's the only thing that will change. That's rarely what happens when you meddle with time. It's why we don't."

An ambulance speeds by.

"I'm having tea now," she says in an almost dreamy tone. "When David dies. Blake is upstairs playing that stupid *Call of Duty* game. My husband, he's at work... God bless him. He's going to be the last to find out, and I'm going to have to tell him."

We sit in silence for what feels like ten minutes, neither of us sure what to say.

"Ask the question that you want to ask, Andre," she urges.

"I don't..."

She holds her hand up, opens a compact mirror with her free hand, and stares into it while dabbing at her eyes. "Take a moment and think. What's the question you want to ask more than anything. Something you've been wondering for the past month? Something I didn't fully answer before? Even if you haven't thought it yet, not consciously at least, you know what it is."

I have no idea what she's talking about. My mind is filled with other things. Dread at having to face Blake again, anger at myself for thinking this would actually work. Pain. Hurt. Fear. All of those things. But a question? What could she...

And then it clicks.

"Why did you pick me?"

She smiles, closing the mirror with a loud click. "There we go," she muses. "Finally, you ask."

Claire turns to me in her seat. The belt slides against her chest and pulls tight with a loud click. She reaches over, placing her hand over my own, and gives me a firm yet soft squeeze.

"I put a lot of pressure on you," she says. "Throwing you into my world and not preparing you. Expecting you to continue our family line. I didn't even ask if you want to—have children, I mean. And I don't need to know. That's not a weight I should put on anyone, not my own children and certainly not you. I take full responsibility for that. For you being here. For not... focusing enough on you."

"And on Blake," I remind her. "He's the one who's suffering. He...feels lost without Dave. His older brother was his guide, no matter how put together he seems." I hesitate, but she squeezes my hand again, a silent confirmation that I should keep going. "He told me all of this because he felt like he couldn't come to you," I say quickly, so I can't take it back. "And there's a reason for that."

"Because I'm prioritizing my own guilt and feelings over my son?" she asks. "Trying, including by bringing you into our family, to keep a piece of David going?"

I hesitate. "Is that a question or..."

"I already know the answer." She smiles, gently moving her hand to my cheek and squeezing it. "I think about that every day. We all deal with grief differently, Andre. I watch my son's last moments over and over again, trying to find a way to keep his memory living on—figuratively and literally. My husband buries himself in his work, in the languages of the past, to distance himself from time travel, and in turn, distance himself from David's memory. And Blake? Blake is trying to fill the hole that his brother left in our family, without being swallowed up by the weight of his memory, and he doesn't even know that, in doing so, he's tearing himself apart."

"So why don't you do something about it?" I ask. "I don't mean that in a bad way."

She chuckles again, softly. "No, of course not. You mean it in the most honest way possible."

She falls silent, sitting back and looking out the window, as if the answer is out there. It's starting to snow, just a bit. Flurries dance in the air, twirling a beautiful ballet as they descend from the heavens.

"I suppose it's because I can control this," she says, gesturing around her. "I know how this story ends. I know what it'll feel like, and I know that, when I want it to, the feeling can be over.

"I cannot control how Blake feels. I can't *fix* that. I can't remove his pain. You tried to. That's not only brave, but also—"

"Stupid?"

"Kind," she says gently. "It's a kindness. Knowing what you'd sacrifice? You only do that for someone you care for. Someone you love."

"I don't know about that," I scoff.

Claire arches a brow. "Really, now? You went through all of this because, what? You're a good person? Come on now, Andre. That's admirable, but foolish. Everyone has some selfishness in them. What you tried to do goes against the rules of human self-preservation. And the only reason humans go against that is because of love.

"He needs someone, Andre. For the longest time, I thought it was me. I thought I could fix everything if I could just…give him space. David was like that. He figured things out on his own, so I assumed that Blake would follow in his footsteps, given the chance. I was wrong."

"I don't…think that's what he wants or needs, though," I say. "I don't think he's looking for you, or anyone, to fix things or try to replace his brother or anything. I think he just wants to feel like there's someone who has his back."

"Someone who will put him first?"

"Exactly."

The quiet settles once more, but it's heavy with a tenseness and tenderness I've never felt. Should I squeeze her shoulder? Let her sit and absorb what I said? I don't turn to face her; that seems wrong, like I'm expecting too much from her.

Eventually, Claire sighs. "I don't know how to do that," she whispers. It seems like it's both terrifying and cathartic for her to admit that. "I don't know how to be that for him. But you obviously do. Case in point: this whole experiment. That's why I wanted him to teach you time traveling, not me. I thought that being close to his brother might give him, in some way, some closure. Help him work through his feelings. Put his anger and hurt to good use."

There's a momentary pause as Claire wrings her hands together.

"I've failed at being his mother, haven't I?"

I shrug. "That's the good thing about being a time traveler, isn't it? We get do-overs."

She smiles, and for the first time, she lets the tears fall down her face. I don't move to comfort her. I just sit there, we both do, in the moment, listening to the faint sounds of the world outside and silently agreeing to never come back here again.

TWENTY-SEVEN

Together, holding hands, Claire and I jump back to 2021, in a gust of wind that makes the living room shudder. The dizzying feeling of returning to the present is worse this time, and my stomach feels like it's in my throat. But I swallow the feeling back and push through it, trying desperately to ignore the pain clawing at my side.

"That was a piggyback jump," she informs me. "You latched on to my jump and came with me. Don't try that with just anyone. Or, better yet, at all." She turns toward the stairs. "Blake," she says with the type of firmness that doesn't leave any room for disagreement. "Come down here. Now."

"Wait, what?" I ask, turning to her. I step in front of her, like that would change anything. "He had nothing to do with this."

"I know."

"Then why are you calling him? I did this on my own. He's been doing what you said, training me."

"Again, I said I know, Andre."

I hear footsteps as he walks across the hallway upstairs and takes the stairs two at a time. Blake's not stupid. He'll know something is up when he sees me down here, especially with his mom. And I don't have time to come up with a good-enough lie by the time he's at the bottom of the steps.

"What's going on?" he asks. "Andre? What are you... Why are you and my mother together?"

My heart rate speeds up. My blood pumps so loudly, I swear it's all I can hear. But Claire's words, as she turns to me, break through the noise.

"Do you want to tell him, or should I?"

"He doesn't need to know," I answer.

"It involves him, since you were doing it for him, Andre. Plus, you can't move forward with him while you're keeping this secret."

"Someone tell me what's going on!"

The ball's in my court. Claire isn't going to save me.

This isn't how I wanted this to go down.

Part of me was hoping that this, as Claire called it, brave kindness would fix everything between us. I don't think that's going to happen anymore.

"I was trying to fix it."

"Fix...what?"

"This. Everything. Dave. Your family. I was—"

But Blake cuts me off, the anger and confusion in his face shifting to understanding. "You did not."

"Oh, he did," says Claire. "He broke rule number two in the process too."

"I thought it was the right thing!"

"Why in the world did you think… Did you think I *wanted* this? Is that what you thought would… What? Make up for what happened on our date?"

Claire feigns disinterest, but I can tell, judging by how her eyebrow quirks, that she's interested—like any parent would be. But she interjects herself, raising her hand like she can control things with a single motion.

But Blake does fall quiet, and I don't speak either.

"What he did was foolish, rash, shortsighted…" she says, looking at Blake, speaking to him. "But his intentions were good."

"I'm furious."

"But he did this for you. Remember that. And in the end, everything will be okay. Nothing was broken. Or rather, nothing will be for long.

"Now, I need to go back in time and make sure that Andre didn't make any…unexpected changes. Can I trust that neither of you will kill each other or try to travel back in time and change something else?"

I want to say yes. No, I want to say, *Yes, ma'am.* But the words won't leave my throat. Blake keeps his gaze firmly fixed on a spot of warped wood on the floor.

"That wasn't a rhetorical question, boys."

"Yes," I say.

"Sure," he replies.

"Good." Claire walks over to me, cupping my cheek again, forcing me to look into her now kind eyes.

Before I can speak, she disappears.

Blake and I stand in silence, letting his mother's aura disappear from the room. It feels like she's still watching us, and if we move too soon, she'll know. Eventually, Blake turns, curtly, heading upstairs with heavy stomps that pulse out his frustration and hurt.

"Blake," I say, hurrying to the base of the steps. "Blake, I'm s—"

"Don't," he orders, standing at the top of the steps, his back to me. He's gripping the railing so tightly that I think his fingers might actually leave marks on the wood when he lets go.

"Did you not hear what your mom said? Did you not *listen*? I was trying to d—"

"I don't care what the reason is!"

He turns so fast that he almost falls off the steps. Angry swatches of red cover his cheeks, and his eyes threaten tears, but he's doing everything he can to hold them back, even if he is failing. This must be the McIntyre way.

He descends the steps again, standing at the bottom of them. There's space between us, but it's filled with his anger and his frustration, pulsing off him like fire off a heated ore.

"Did you even think before you jumped? How long have you been planning this? Did you consider who you'd hurt? What could go wrong? How you could *die*? Did you even care? That's not romantic! That's not sweet and generous! It's *selfish* and *stupid*!"

Each sentence is like a knife, with pinpoint accuracy, reminding me with each word how I messed up. But it wasn't just that—it was how I hurt him, how he felt like I betrayed him in some way. And that hurt more than the shame.

"I can understand, logically, what you thought you were doing," Blake says while pacing back and forth. "But emotionally? Did you even stop to think, for one freakin' second, about me?"

"I did this *for* you!" I insist.

"Really? What would have happened to us if I forgot about you? If you forgot about me? I wanted us to try. What if things changed? Time travel *does* that, Andre! It changes things in ways you can never understand, like my mom said. And if getting Dave back was something that I *wanted*, I could have asked her to do that a long time ago!"

"You know that wasn't..."

"No, Andre! I don't know. I don't freaking know, because what I thought I *did* know was that I could trust you. And look where that got me!"

I narrow my eyes and ball my fists by my side to still my anger. Blake needs this. He needs to rant and feel...well, whatever he feels...about my failed attempt to change the past.

"I did everything I could, Blake," I say quietly. "You might not understand, but I was trying to do the right thing."

"That's the thing about *trying* to do something, Andre. You either do it, or you don't. There is no try."

He lets out a deep breath. "Just leave. Go home."

"I can try again," I whisper. "I...I can still fix this. I know I can."

"Stop trying to be something you're not. You're not a time

traveler; you're just someone who stumbled into it. And you know what? You're the worst type of time traveler—someone who does more harm than good."

Each word hurts. Each syllable is like a needle finding my weak spot and jabbing in deep.

But before I can fight or fly, a surge of pain, worse than before, sharp and deep, stabs at my stomach. I double over, grabbing my body and almost buckling to my knees. I squeeze my eyes shut, and all I see are stars, colorful stars, black stars, white stars. It's like I can see, in this brief moment, almost every color. There's a ringing in my head that sounds like every cell in my body screaming all at once. It drowns out everything, even my own inner voice.

When I open my eyes after the worst of the pain stops, I'm no longer in Blake's house. I'm outside.

And there's snow on the ground.

As the colors all around me start to come together and objects take form, it's clear to me where I am. I'm in Boston, at the edge of an alley, a familiar one based on the street signs I see across the street.

Someone bumps into me. Someone familiar, despite the longer hair, dingy clothes, sharper stubble, and darkened features on his face.

Someone who is just as surprised to see me as I am to see him.

"Andre?" Michael gasps.

TWENTY-EIGHT

I've seen many versions of Michael since jumping through time, but never a version like this.

His face is sullen, his skin a shade grayer than before. His hair is longer and unkempt. Matted. Jaggedly cut. He reminds me of pieces of a puzzle that don't fully come together to make a complete person. Like something is missing.

The light in his eyes is gone. And I didn't know how much I missed it, truly missed it, until now.

"So," he says, rubbing his nose with his sleeve. "You came back, huh?"

I reach forward to grab him, but he moves back, far enough that he's unreachable. Farther than he's ever been before, even through time and space.

"Do you remember what happened when you last left? What you said? Do you even know what year it was then?"

"Nineteen seventy."

"And now?"

I can't answer that one, and he knows it. He sucks on his teeth in disgust.

"Seventy-three. It's been three years."

I do a quick mental check. What do I know about 1973? We don't learn much about the seventies in school. Maybe I should have done some research before I left.

But every other time I'd always had Michael by my side. It had been us versus the world or creating our own world.

Not anymore.

"You left," he seethes. "You left me, and you didn't care, and you just went off to do whatever it is you went to do. I thought I'd never see you again. Every day, I woke up and felt both happy and furious that I remembered you. Remembered us. I kept waiting to forget you. I wish I could forget you."

He turns his back to me, walking away with hurried but sporadic steps. And, like always, I follow.

"I went to fix things."

"Yeah, right."

"Seriously! Michael. Michael!"

I grab his shoulder, and in that moment, that fraction of a second, that quiver of a heartbeat, I see a side of him I never thought I'd see.

"Don't. Touch. Me," he hisses. "Don't you ever touch me again. Don't you ever…"

He growls, an animalistic groan that comes from deep within his stomach. He runs his fingers through his shaggy hair.

For the first time since I met Michael, I feel something new: fear.

And I have to push through it.

"What happened to you?"

Slowly, Michael pulls himself out of his own mind and turns to me with a wild fury in his eyes. "What happened to me." He says it like a statement. "You want to know that badly?"

Michael takes a step forward, and in response, I take a step back.

"After you left, went off to save that boy of yours, I waited to forget you. But I didn't. And I thought maybe I had lost my mind. And you were never really real. It messed me up. I didn't want to remember. So I had to try to forget you. And what better way to forget someone than in the bottom of a bottle?"

He doesn't say it like he's ashamed.

"One drink turned to two, two turned to four, and well, the past three years started to feel like a blur."

Just by looking at him, I know he's been self-medicating with more than alcohol. I don't know what drugs he's on, but he's on something.

I swallow thickly, forcing myself to speak. "What about your family?" I ask.

"Seriously? That's what you're thinking about right now?"

But his posture relaxes, even if just a fraction. He takes half a step back, and I feel my breath return. I let out a breath I didn't even know I had been holding.

"My parents don't want anything to do with me."

"What about your work? With the paper? Or your music? You always cared about that."

"I sold my guitar...what? A year ago?" He shrugs. "Maybe

two. You don't have a right to judge me. No one has the fucking right."

I feel like I'm drowning, watching every good moment we spent together disappear into an endless darkness of oblivion.

"I can fix this," I say quietly.

"You still don't get it. No matter what you do, you still don't fucking get it."

I feel a sense of weightlessness as I wait, where anything is possible, when he could say or do anything.

"Not everything is about you, Andre. My life is my own. You can't just go back and 'fix' me. Who do you think you are?"

"I didn't—" I sputter.

"No. Shut up. It's my turn to talk. Not yours. This is my life now. This is who I am. Maybe it's not someone you want to be with. Maybe it's not who you thought I'd be. But you know what? Screw you. I wish I'd never met you."

"Michael…" I want to tell him to stop. I want to tell him I'm sorry. To say so many things. To apologize, explain how wrong I was. But there's an invisible wall between us, with a complex lock that I don't know how to pick.

And there's a familiar, growing pain.

I can fix this, I think. I can fix this. Screw what Claire said. This is worth fixing. I won't be the cause of this. I won't be the cause of hurting someone so pure, so good. This won't be his destiny.

But before I can do anything else, a pain unlike anything I've felt before pierces my side.

I can't tell up from down, left from right. Colors blur together, and every sense is going haywire. Is Michael grabbing my shoulder? I can't tell. Is he speaking my name? Does he sound worried, or is that my imagination?

There are only three things I know for sure.

Pain.

Blackness.

And a desire to die. A desire so strong, I barely feel my body hit the floor before that darkness swallows me whole.

TWENTY-NINE

When I wake, I'm not fully conscious. I can hear words. Mom's voice. A doctor that's not familiar. All slices of a giant movie reel stitched together in the most inconvenient of ways.

My body won't respond to my commands. *Blink. Move. Scream. Twitch.* Nothing. It's like my orders are sent out and shot down in space, disappearing into vast nothingness, leaving me at the mercy of whatever this is. I have no idea how much time goes by before I finally wake up, but when I do, I can tell it's mid to late afternoon. The sun through the window is low on the horizon.

The first person I see when I open my eyes is Mom. She's chewing on her nails, talking with the doctor—a woman with a tight bun and light brown skin—with a worried expression on her face. Dad's back is to me, but I see him nodding frantically, causing his whole body to shake. It's as if none of them expect me to wake up.

But the look on the doctor's face isn't concern.

I like her.

"He's awake," Blake says.

I turn my head and see him. He's not sitting in the chair next to me but standing by the window, his arms crossed stiffly. His eyes don't stay on mine for long; he quickly turns away.

I try to open my mouth to speak, but before I can, Mom, Dad, and Mr. and Mrs. McIntyre crowd around me (to Mom and Dad's surprise).

"Baby," Mom breathes out, kissing my cheeks and forehead more times than I think she's ever done. "You gave us a scare. Are you okay? What happened? Are you hurt? Do you feel any pain?"

"You gave us a fright, son," Dad says in that way that's softly scolding but actually caring.

Claire and Greg say nothing, but the look on their faces says it all.

Concern. Unbridled concern.

The doctor squeezes past Mom and Dad, standing by my side. She pulls out her stethoscope, placing the cold metal against my chest.

"I'm Dr. Kapoor. How are you feeling, Andre?" she asks, moving it from spot to spot.

"Cold," I whisper.

"We'll get some blankets for you. Any headache? Stomachache? Dizziness? Pain?"

"Abdomen," I say as confidently as I can. Maybe that'll make them think I'm not hurting as much as I am. When, in fact, everything—every nerve—hurts.

I don't want to think what is screaming in my head. If I think it, I'll say it, and if I say it, that might make it a reality.

"Is his body rejecting the liver?" Mom says it for me.

Dr. Kapoor doesn't answer at first. She checks my chart, the machines, her watch, and then a few other vitals before turning to my parents.

"It's not that simple." When she sees their reaction, she quickly adds, "But I want to run some more tests on Andre. See what we're dealing with. If it is, and that is the worst-case scenario, we caught it early. We can give him drugs and hopefully reverse the effects."

"Hopefully?" Dad asks. "And, by the way, where is…"

"Dr. Moore? She's serving at another hospital for the week. I've been fully briefed on Andre's condition, and I'm confident that I can step in here," Dr. Kapoor says without missing a beat. "There's nothing you can do for Andre right now, except give him his rest. I'll have more information for you tomorrow. How about you go and get some dinner or coffee, and we can talk more in, say, an hour?"

Mom and Dad aren't buying it. Both of them shifted their whole lives around when I got sick. It was always me and them against this cancer. Why change that?

"I'll be fine," I promise. "Just get some food and relax."

They hesitate for a moment before Claire comes in for the kill.

"I know Dr. Kapoor personally," she says soothingly. "I went to college with her. How about we talk about her credentials over some dinner, hmm?"

There it is. Mom's shoulders relax. Dad nods curtly. He gives my shoulder a squeeze before walking out with Greg. Mom gives me a kiss before whispering, "If you need anything, call me."

Blake follows, and knowing that I can't call her without a phone, places mine on the table next to me. We lock eyes for a moment, and he smiles, though it's fragile.

"You're in good hands with Dr. Kapoor," he vows.

I want to tell Blake to stay—or, at least, ask him to—but before I can muster up the strength, he's gone, leaving me and Dr. Kapoor alone.

She doesn't look up from her clipboard at first. I reach over to grab my phone, but my arms feel like lead. Dr. Kapoor glances up, walks over, and hands it to me.

"Now I can ask you the real questions I wanted to ask," she says, pulling a chair close to my bed. "Are you feeling groggy? Tingling feeling all over? Heavy? Dizzy?"

I nod to each one of them.

"I'm a time traveler," she says. "Just like Mr. and Mrs. McIntyre, and just like you. They brought me in to deal with your…unique situation." She smiles softly.

It's not the type of smile that's reassuring.

"What's happening to me?" I whisper, the scratchiness in my throat burning like hot dragon fire. "Everything feels…"

"Painful?" she asks, not looking up. "In the most simplistic of terms, your body is rejecting your liver."

I can feel the speed of my blood increasing. The panic starting to rise. Rejection is the one thing we've all been trying to avoid.

What are the chances of another liver coming around, or even someone who is a perfect match who'd actually be willing to donate part of their liver to me? Minimal. Can you live without a liver? No.

I let out a shuddered breath and close my eyes tightly. If I keep them tightly shut for long enough, I can fight back the hot tears starting to form. If I can push them back long enough, then I can do what I do best: come up with a plan. Strategize. Evaluate and then execute.

"What are the next steps?" I ask, eyes still closed.

I hear Dr. Kapoor wheel her chair next to me and feel her press a warm hand to my shoulder. It's not to comfort me but to get my attention.

Eventually, I open my eyes and look over at her.

"It's simple, really. There's no medical intervention that you need. No pills." She taps my chest softly. "Just you. This one's on you, Andre.

"Your time traveling is what's causing the rejection," she explains. "It happens sometimes with people like you. Individuals who are gifted the ability to time travel, not those who are born with it. The body rejects the ability. In simple terms? Traveling is ripping your genes apart with an intensity that the liver cannot compensate for.

"Well, you didn't ease into that at all," I say almost coldly. I should feel something more, but right now, the words just feel hollow. I'm sure I'll react later. "Anything else?"

She doesn't need to say it. I know what she's going to say.

"I can't time travel anymore," I finish for her.

Dr. Kapoor nods, writing some notes. "Traveling aggravates your system. You stop traveling, and the pain—and the risk—will go away. I'm going to hold you overnight, give you some pills for the pain, and…"

"And if I don't?"

She pauses, her pencil stopping in what looks like the middle of a loop. She slowly glances up, only raising her eyes, not her head.

"You refuse to stop, and it won't only be your liver that your body rejects, Andre," she warns. "Your whole body will shut down. You're effectively ripping yourself apart whenever you jump. That's what's causing your body to short-circuit. It's starting with your liver because that's the source. But it won't end there."

"Are you sure?" I ask. "Medicine isn't—"

"I'm sure," she interrupts sternly.

Dr. Kapoor puts the clipboard down and focuses her gaze on me in a way that makes it impossible for me to look away. It's hypnotizing and threatening all at once.

"Let me make it clear for you. If you continue to time travel, you will be lucky if you can speak, let alone walk. Eventually, you will rip yourself apart in a way that nothing—absolutely nothing—can put back together."

Dr. Kapoor moves to leave, assuming that this final statement is enough to make me understand the severity of my situation. I get it. In many ways, I'm worse off than I was before the transplant.

"Get some rest, Andre. Right now, that's all you need to focus on."

THIRTY

School is out of the question, but I'm not worried about that right now. Mom and Dad aren't either. They're back to worrying about my health. Which is good for me.

Now I have bigger problems to deal with. Well, two bigger problems.

The pain is gone within the first three days. But my eagerness to get up and get moving—to be doing *something*—makes me strain my muscles, forcing my parents to remind me that staying in bed wasn't just a suggestion.

Lying here, doing nothing, is against my nature. There are so many things I should be doing right now, but my body has other plans. Sit. Wait. And recover.

That's all it's been doing for almost a year. Waiting. Hoping. Pining.

When do I get to take charge of my own life? When do I get to be in control of my future?

And I can't stop thinking about my last meeting with Michael. Michael, who loved life and music and wanted to fight for gay rights. For all I know, he could be dead. I guess I could try to find him, see what happened to him. But I can't bring myself to do it, to know what outcome I might have caused.

But maybe I could change things. With just one more jump. Just ten more minutes.

A soft knock on my door turns my attention away from my own dark thoughts. Mom pushes her head in. "How are you feeling?"

I shrug. "Fine," I say, sitting up. My abs hurt far less than before. I can walk around and do most things by myself. "Wish I could eat some solid food, though."

"Next week," she promises, slipping in. "Then you can have whatever you want."

"You know the problem is with my liver, right? Not my stomach? I didn't have stomach cancer."

"I know what type of cancer my son had, Andre," Mom quips back.

"And trust me, so do I. Considering I'm the one who lived with it and have a body that might be worse off for it."

She lets out a frustrated sigh and takes in a deep breath. She pauses, looking anywhere but at me. I know she feels tense; I feel it too. It's like it's not the same between us anymore. Moms can detect when their children are different. I'm sure it's some evolved sense of awareness or something. The usual suspects—drugs, alcohol, skipping school—those don't apply here. She knows something is up, but she can't place it, and she'll never be able to.

I wish I could tell her. Tell her the truth, have her and Dad support me in this like they did with my cancer. But I can't do that to them. They wouldn't understand.

But right now, I'd kill for her advice. To know what she'd think I should do. She always has the best advice. The simplest of sentences to solve my problems or at least steer me in the right direction.

Maybe someday.

"You have a visitor," she says softly and steps aside. Half a beat passes before I hear shuffling. I expect Isobel; she's been texting me nonstop. But instead, it's Blake.

"Hey," he says, waving meekly, half hidden behind my mom. She quirks her brow, a silent exchange that he's unable to see, asking if I want her to tell him to leave.

And, for a moment, I think about it. But curiosity gets the better of me, as it always does. Isn't that what's gotten me into trouble these past few months?

"He can stay."

Mom nods and steps aside. "I'll be downstairs if you want or need anything," she says, talking to me, but I know the offer extends to both of us.

I listen to the sound of her footsteps retreating. Blake stands in the doorway, unmoving.

"You can sit." I gesture to the chair by my desk. He nods and closes the door behind him.

Blake doesn't just sit; he collapses, his whole body *thumping* down into the chair. His shoulders, usually perfectly straight, slouch slightly, and his gaze doesn't focus clearly on me. It doesn't focus on anything, really. It's like he doesn't know where to look or what to say.

"Me too," I say, breaking the silence.

"What?"

"Me too," I repeat. "I'm not sure what to say either."

"Are you...okay?"

I shrug, shifting toward him with a hiss. "I haven't jumped, if that's what you're asking, so I think I'm fine? Still sore. Mom and Dad are hovering over me like hawks, which I thought I was done with."

"I get that." He nods. "I mean, rejection is nothing to take lightly or ignore."

"If only they really understood it."

"If only."

Silence fills the room again, but it's not quiet, it's loud. There's so much unsaid between Blake and me that even the stillness is filled with words. Who should speak first? What should either of us say? We've both said things to each other that we regret. We both talk too much, act first, and don't think.

"I'm glad you're okay," Blake says. "Truly, Andre. I'm glad. I was...worried. And I'm sorry about how I acted before. I never should have spoken to you like that. I hope you can forgive me."

I open my mouth to say, *Really?* But I can tell, when I see his face, that he's speaking the truth. There's heaviness in his eyes, a dark weight that reads like fear and guilt.

Guilt that he's responsible.

Fear of losing me.

"Hey," I say, swinging my legs over the side of my bed. My bare feet touch the floor. I stand up, ignoring the pain and swallowing a hiss, but I don't make it more than one step before Blake's gently pushing me back.

"Get back in bed, Andre."

"Not until you hear me."

"I'm going to call your mother up here, I swear to God. Get back in bed."

I study his eyes, trying to gauge how much I can push back. The rigidness of his jaw tells me there's no wiggle room.

"It's not your fault," I say, sitting down. "And I forgive you. We both made a lot of mistakes."

Blake looks down at his feet, tapping his right foot against the wood in a beat I don't recognize. It's a metronome, of sorts, and the only constant sound in the room for half a dozen passing moments.

"Remember what we agreed on when we first started this? That I'd teach you how to time travel, and you'd grant me one free request? Remember that?"

My body tenses. "I remember," I say quickly. "But—"

Blake looks up at me, and his foot falls still. "I've decided what I want to ask you to do," he interrupts. "I want us to try, Andre. To really try. You and me, if you'll have me again. No do-overs, because I don't believe in those. But I want us to see if what I think there is between us, this feeling... I want us to see if it can become something, you know? If you and I can become something. That's what I want. A chance for us. But I only want it if you want it. And I don't want to be your second choice. I don't want you to be with me because you can't be with him. So… What do you think?"

I think about it. I think about a future, not only my own but a future with Blake. A life together, with ups and downs, highs and lows. Maybe I'm just daydreaming, or maybe I'm being too optimistic, but it feels so real, so tangible.

And, judging by the way my breath hitches, I want it. I want it badly.

"I can give you that," I finally say.

Blake's sharp features turn into a wide smile, one that reflects in his eyes.

"Really? You're not joking? Oh, shit." He laughs nervously. "I thought you'd say no! I seriously had a whole speech planned!"

"I thought I just heard your speech?"

"I had even more. I *rehearsed* it. Be honored."

A throaty laugh leaves my mouth. "I'm going to need to hear that someday. But first…I need to do something."

"Anything," he says without hesitation.

He's not going to be that eager once he hears what I'm thinking.

"I need to go back, Blake," I whisper, so quietly that I'm not sure I even say it. "One more time."

"Andre…you know…"

"I know."

"The risk you'd be taking."

"I know."

Blake looks at me.

"I need to say goodbye. We left on such bad terms. I need to make sure he's okay if I'm going to let him go."

I expect him to say no. I'm ready for it. I wouldn't blame him; he just got me back, I'm alive, and what would saying goodbye do for me, anyway? All reasonable answers. All logical answers.

But what I'm doing, what I am, isn't logical anymore. It's emotional, it's feelings, it's biochemical reactions fueling my motives in ways I didn't know were possible. And I know this is something I need to do.

And I want Blake's support while I do it.

Blake sighs, running his fingers through his hair. Slowly, he takes my right hand into his left one. Then he puts my left hand over his and puts his right hand on top. He leans forward, resting his forehead against mine, his eyes closed.

"Make me your tether," he says. "Think of me when you go, think of me when you want to return. I'll be here for you. I'll be there with you. I'll make sure you come back in one piece. I promise you."

Is this really happening? I hesitate, waiting for Blake to change his mind, to come to his senses. But as he pulls his forehead back and smiles, that warm, boyish smile, I know he's not going to. I know he's in this for the long haul.

I kiss his knuckles, letting my lips linger. "I'll come back; I promise."

He nods. "I trust you."

THIRTY-ONE

Pain. So much freaking pain. The worst I've had so far.

It doesn't feel like before. It's not a searing or a throbbing pain but a type of surge that takes over every inch of my body. My bones, my muscles, my cells, even my hair and nails feel like they hurt. It feels like every cell is being ripped apart.

It takes me a moment to realize that I'm lying on a cool floor. The cold feels nice against my warm skin, and when I force myself up to my hands and knees, I can tell I'm drenched in sweat. My stomach heaves, twice actually, but no vomit comes up, and for that, I'm thankful.

My body feels like lead as I stand, and I'm lucky that there's a counter for me to grab on to when I slip. The walls are a beige color, and there's a painting of a sailboat looking back at me. It takes all the energy I have to focus on it. Michael's apartment. I'm in the right place, and I can only hope it's the right time.

Someone says my name. The voice is muddled, like they are speaking through water and I'm at the bottom of the sea, but I can make out those two syllables. It's a man's voice, and he puts a hand on my shoulder. I'd know that touch anywhere.

Michael.

He helps me stand up and helps me walk to the couch, although it's more like he's carrying me. I focus my vision on him as best I can, but there are five different versions of him, all spinning around a center version. It takes all the energy I have to make the versions come into one.

And that says nothing of how my body feels like it's not my own.

"I'm going to get you some water," he says. I can make out that much. My head lobs back and rests against the couch.

Focus, Andre, I demand. *Focus on why you're here. Focus on the roughness of the couch. Focus on each drop of sweat that trickles down your body.*

Focus on anything other than the pain.

Because if I focus on that, I'll want to scream—and I probably will. Or cry, or even die.

Can someone die from pain? Who knows.

When Michael returns, my body is a little better. All, or at least most, of my cylinders are firing. I can make Michael out. His voice sounds clearer, and the concern on his face? That's evident.

"Hey," I say quietly.

"Hey," he says back. He raises his hand and strokes my cheek. "First of all, before I say anything else, I want to say I'm sorry. You don't have to forgive me, but I need to say it.

Second of all, what did you do." It's a question but spoken like a statement.

"How long have I been gone?"

He looks over at the clock. "Almost twenty-four hours exactly. Long enough for me to calm down and understand how stupid I was."

I take a slow drink of water, and the cool liquid feels like heaven against my burning throat. It takes effort to drink—something I've never experienced before—and it makes me envious of each time that breathing, talking, *thinking* came easily to me.

"You have nothing to be sorry about," I say once I put the water down. "I said things I shouldn't have said too."

He grins—that adorable, charming lopsided grin. "So we're both idiots, then, huh?"

"I can agree to that." I smile back.

His hand doesn't move from my cheek, stroking it soothingly. It's nice, I have to admit. It almost makes me forget why I'm here, why I came all this way, why I risked this.

But even as I look at Michael, all I can think about is Blake.

"Do you need more water?" Michael asks, seeing that I've finished it. "Or do you want something else, something harder?"

"Probably not the best idea."

"No…" A beat passes. "Probably not."

He doesn't move from his position kneeling in front of me, but slowly, he pulls back his hand. "You never answered my question."

No, I didn't. Is it because I don't want to? Is it because I'm afraid that, once I do, it'll all be real, and I can't take it back? As I sit here in the past with Michael, I can imagine a future. No, not imagine. That future could still be a reality. A possibility we both can have, no matter how small the chance.

Once I do what I'm here to do, that door closes. But maybe, just maybe, that's not a bad thing.

I pat the spot next to me on the couch. Slowly, Michael slides up and sits. There's no space between us, my right leg and his left one touching. I think he needs that connection. I think, deep down, he knows something is coming. Something he's not going to like.

Maybe that'll make this easier.

"There's something I need to tell you," I say slowly. "No, that's not right. There are some *things* I need to tell you."

"Well, at least you didn't start this conversation with 'we need to talk.'" He grins nervously.

I force a smile on my face, but I'm not sure it's convincing. I'm not really sure of anything right now. Am I making the right choice? Am I taking the easy way out? Is there another solution?

Maybe if I had more time. Maybe if there wasn't so much at stake, I could find another solution. I could research, I could experiment, I could do so many different things.

But, if I've learned one thing from all of this, it's that I'm not a scientist. No matter how much my parents want me to be one or how good I am at science or any of those logical reasons and pieces of evidence that point to it, that's not who I am.

And it's time for me to stop thinking like that and to start thinking the right way, the only way I should be thinking; Andre's way.

"I want you to know I love you, Michael," I say. I think that's important to start with. "I love you so much. The few days—"

"Years," he says, correcting me—again with that lopsided smile. Except this time, he nudges my leg with his own to remind me that he's joking. I make sure to nudge back.

"Years," I repeat. "The past few years have been amazing, Michael. Some of the best years I've ever had."

"Me too," he agrees. Slowly, he slides his hand across the space between us and intertwines his fingers with mine, squeezing them. The connection grounds me, and in that fraction of a second, everything else fades away, and only Michael sits in front of me.

I swallow the discomfort that feels like trying to swallow smoke or water, and I say the thing I've come here to say.

"This is the last time I can see you."

The words, all nine of them, feel like bullets leaving my mouth. I watch as they strike Michael.

"What do you mean?" he asks. "You're here with me right now. Are you still planning on going through with saving Dave? Even if you do, maybe we can still be with each other. Don't you think there's a way?"

"Maybe…but not for us."

"Love is never simple," he argues. "You have to fight for it, Dre. It's not just going to present itself to you and be perfect all the time. It's a struggle."

"If I had a choice, I'd be with you. I need you to remember that. No matter what, even if you're angry with me for the rest of your life, I need you to know that if it was just about how much…how much I love you, then I would stay.

"But that's not the only factor here." I raise my shirt a bit, showing him my scar. It's red, and when I bring his hand over to touch it, his fingers recoil from the warmth.

"What…"

"Jumping is tearing me apart, Michael," I admit. "I don't know how. I don't know why. But it is."

Slowly, his fingers trace the jagged scar, with soft palpations. The flesh is sore, but I don't make a sound or react. This might be the last time he touches me.

"How bad does it hurt?" he mutters.

Part of me thinks about lying, but the truth will set you free, right?

"A lot." I don't tell him that I don't know what will happen when I jump back. This jump felt like I was being ripped between the past and the present. The next one…

I can't think about that right now. It doesn't help anyone to dwell on that. This moment is about Michael. It's about me. It's about saying goodbye.

"And this happens each time you jump?"

I nod. He's putting two and two together. I can see the gears turning behind his eyes. He's understanding what this means for me. He's weighing the pros and cons of selfishness, thinking about what will happen if he asks me to stay.

And I hope he doesn't. But at the same time, I hope he does.

Because if he does, I'll find a way to stay. I know I will, no matter how stupid it is.

"I want you to know that if there were any other way, I would stay," I whisper, feeling my throat close, like it's trying to keep me from continuing to say what I know I have to.

"I know," he whispers, squeezing my hand in his. "I'm not mad."

"You should be."

"Why?" he asks. "I wouldn't want you to hurt yourself for me, Dre. What type of person would that make me? When you care about someone, you want what's best for them. You want them to be safe and happy."

"I am happy when I'm with you," I argue.

"Oh, babe," he whispers, stroking my cheek again. He presses his lips gently against my forehead. His lips stay pressed against my flesh, like he's marking my skin with his touch. "Do me a favor," he says when he pulls back. "Just one thing."

"Anything," I promise.

"Be happy. Find a way to be happy. Don't stop living. Don't wallow or stay in bed or whatever you boys do in the future. Promise me that."

"I promise," I swear. "But you have to promise to do the same. Keep up with your music. Write a book. All of those things. Live your life. Whatever form it takes."

"Oh, I most definitely will," he says confidently. "I mean,

who knows, maybe in school you'll be assigned to read my great American novel. See what you're passing up on, Dre? The next…"

"Joan Didion?"

He grins and nods slowly. "Exactly."

"I'm serious, Michael. You have to promise me that no matter what happens, you'll keep working hard," I urge. "I've seen your—"

Michael holds his hand up. "If you're going to say you've seen my future, I don't want to know."

"But—"

He shakes his head. "No, Andre. Seriously. That's for me to find out, not for me to know. And who knows, maybe it won't happen. The future isn't set in stone, right? And I'm pretty sure you shouldn't be trying to change the past anyway, yeah?"

"Rule number three," I recite.

"Exactly. So how about this? You let me walk my path. You'll walk yours. And we'll just enjoy this moment and not worry about the future. Deal?"

"Deal."

This moment is all that matters. We don't need anything else. Well, we need more time. But we can't have that. This, though? This is good.

"We'll see each other again, yeah?" I ask. "Even if you're in your seventies. I'll still visit you."

"Oh God, no." He laughs. "You are not going to visit me in a nursing home. I forbid it. Part of being happy is living your life, Dre. Not waiting until you can see me. You don't need that. Keep our memories close. Cherish them. Let them fuel you to do whatever you want to do. But don't let them fester. Memories shouldn't be a poison.

"Here," he says, getting up. "I'll help you." Michael walks over to his record player. He sifts through a dozen records before finding one and putting it on. Slowly, music fills the air as he comes back over. He sits and grabs my shoulder, guiding my head into his lap.

"Who is this?"

"Doesn't matter," he says. "From now on, it's our album. And once the album is over, you're going to leave, okay? Go and live your life like you promised. And I will do the same, okay?"

I can't answer. I want to answer. I want to agree. But nothing comes out of my mouth. Because once I say "okay," it's true.

"Okay?" he repeats.

Finally the word forms. "Okay."

Michael and I sit quietly. We listen to the music, let it flood our bodies. For the whole album, easily an hour long, neither of us speak. His fingers trace through my short 'fro. My fingers stroke his thigh.

And it's perfect. It's absolutely perfect.

Until the record ends, and the air falls silent.

"Time to go," he whispers, gently sitting me up. His fingers smooth my shirt, adjust my collar, and run through my hair one more time. I look at his face for the first time since he put my head down, and for the last time…

And I notice that he's crying. Not loud, sobbing tears, but silent ones, soft trickles. Streaky lines on his face tell me he's been crying for a while.

"Time to go," I repeat.

Something tells me I should kiss him. That's probably the right thing to do when you're not going to see someone again.

But instead, we hug, wrapping ourselves around each other as tightly as possible.

"Before I go, I want to say one—"

"I know, Andre Cobb from Boston, I know," he says before I can say it.

We stay in that position, just holding each other, for I don't know how long. I don't care either. Instead, I focus on the feeling of his skin against mine. His scent. His breathing. Anything and everything I can hold on to. I want to remember it, to cherish it, to never forget.

My heart is pounding in my chest so hard that I think I'm going to pass out. This doesn't feel the way a jump feels; this feels different. This feels like an emotional high. Like joy and anger and hurt and fear all at once.

It feels good and bad and real and false and like something I want and something I want to stay as far away from as possible.

And it's exactly what I need to push through the pain that erupts the moment I think about jumping back to the present. My present.

It's what I need to go home. My home. My real home. My real life.

And to live it like Michael did: to the fullest.

And that's exactly what I'm going to do.

When I return, Blake is still on my bed.

That was, and most likely will be, the most important seventy-five minutes of my life.

I wonder if it will be the most important seventy-five seconds of his.

Blake looks up, smiling nervously. "Hey," he whispers. "You okay?"

I don't think *okay* is the right word. There are so many other appropriate expressions to describe how I feel.

Broken.

Shattered.

Exhausted.

Defeated.

But none of those come out. Instead, I wrap my arms as tightly as I can around Blake, as if to test whether he's real, and I cry—I cry so hard my whole body shakes.

And Blake? He just holds me, and he doesn't say a word.

10 MONTHS LATER

THIRTY-TWO

"Babe! Come on! I swear to God, if you don't come out here right now, I'm going to watch the season finale of *Heroes* without you!"

I roll my eyes. There's no way to know if Blake is telling the truth or not, but something like that? He might just do it. And he knows I've been dying to get his reactions to a show he barely understood. Watching his face and having to pause the show every five minutes to explain what was going on was more fun than actually watching the show.

But, this is his graduation party, and it is, after all, his day. What the prince wants, the prince gets.

"I need to go see what he wants," I tell Isobel, giving her the rest of my cake as I jump off the stool. "Finish this for me?"

Isobel shakes her head, her bangles clicking. "Absolutely not. I'm not going to eat all those carbs right before I leave for my internship in Italy! It's like you don't even know me!"

"I know you always have and always will look beautiful."

"You're supposed to say that. You're my best friend, *and* you know that if you're not nice to me before I leave for Milan and my plane crashes and I die, you'll hate yourself forever."

I pause, staring at her. "After all these years, I still feel like I don't know you."

She flips her hair teasingly. "I'm a puzzle, darling. Besides, your job as my best friend is just to understand me and accept me for who I am, not judge me or fix me or give me advice. That job is for a therapist or a psychiatrist, which you are not."

"Not *yet*."

"You don't even *want* to be a doctor anymore!"

I shrug. Who knows what life will bring? I've become more comfortable with that reality. Finding solace in the unknown. "Still. Did you hear what you just said? You're going to Milan, not a war zone."

"Honestly, biotech can be a cutthroat business."

I roll my eyes and hold up my index finger, telling her I'll be back in a minute, before weaving through the McIntyre house. There are a lot of people here—mostly Blake's family, some friends from both of our schools, and fellow time travelers who know the McIntyres. They nod to me, tip their glasses, squeeze my shoulder—small signs to let me know that they know who I am and what I'm about.

It's almost as if they're on my side. Maybe they are, and I feel a sense of weightlessness knowing that.

I move into the backyard, where music is playing. Mom and Dad are talking to Mr. and Mrs. McIntyre, chatting in what seems like a friendly way.

"Took them long enough," I mutter, waving to them as I walk out. Mom smiles. Claire raises her glass. Dad and Greg just nod. When I walk by them, I pick up a bit of their conversation.

"Brown has a good history program," Greg says. "Maybe Andre would be interested in that? I can put in a good word."

"Would you? That would be great. We've been thinking about taking a few college tours. Andre's shown interest in political science and sociology too. We're trying to put together a good list of schools for those programs."

"Harvard and Tufts both have great programs."

"I know, but I think he wants to make his own choice on this one. If he wants to stay close to home, that's great. But we're not going to force him."

I don't expect they'll be throwing any joint parties anytime soon, but at least Mom is willing to put up with them. She still blames them for me not finishing my summer school classes, which is the reason I'm being held back a year. She blames Blake for being the reason why I'm no longer interested in medicine, but she understands, finally, that it's my choice and that my future is my own.

Of course, she can never know the truth, and everyone has chosen to respect that. Sometimes a small lie is the best option.

"Dre!" Blake screams from the yard.

Oh my God! "I'm coming, I'm coming, Jesus."

"I'm not Jesus, but…"

"Blake, if you finish that sentence…" warns Claire.

I take the steps from the porch two at a time and meet him

in the grassy yard. Blake and his cousins, who are at least half his age, are playing some modified game of tag that doesn't make any sense at first glance. But when one of the curly-haired boys touches me, the other kids gasp.

"You're the monster now!" says a girl with half her teeth missing.

"The what?"

"The monster, Andre," Blake says, not clarifying things at all. "Come on, learn the rules. You know. *The monster*."

The girl pulls back and starts running wildly, with no reasonable pattern to her movements. The other kids do the same thing.

"This is what you called me over for?"

Blake crosses his arms over his chest in that indignant way and scoffs. "I'll have you know, Monster is a very important game."

Before I can say anything, his arms slip around my waist, and he pulls me close. Our lips collide and find their familiar place against one another. It's been ten months, and his kisses still make me shiver.

"You never have a problem when I'm a monster in bed," he whispers against me.

"Blake!" I roar, shoving him to put some space between us before lunging at him, aiming my hands at the secret ticklish spots I've learned over the life of our relationship. Smirking, he jumps just out of reach. I don't need him to tell me that my cheeks are burning. I can feel it.

Thank God for being Black.

"I'm going to get you, Blake," I growl playfully, taking a step forward.

"Before you do whatever it is you're going to do to my son, which I fully endorse, by the way, can you come upstairs, Andre?" Claire says from the top of the steps. She's leaning against the railing, her sundress billowing, a faint smile on her face.

"Mom! You'd be Andre's accomplice?"

"I have no idea what you're talking about," she says and winks. "Andre?"

"Coming." I turn to Blake as I walk backward. "I'll be right back."

"Don't be a stranger." He smiles, blowing a kiss.

"Never with you."

I stop for a moment, kissing Mom on the cheek before heading inside. I know the McIntyre house like the back of my hand now, having spent almost 140 days here in the past ten months. Claire leads me down the hallway and into the study, sliding the cherry doors closed behind me.

"I just wanted to take a moment for the two of us," she smiles, gesturing to the couch. It's the same couch I sat on the first time I came here. "Thirsty?"

"Water is fine. I wouldn't be here without you, you know."

"Alive or…?" She hands me a bottle from the cooler, taking one for herself.

"With Blake, I mean. And an ex–time traveler."

She shrugs, sitting down next to me. "Soul mates," she says simply.

"Sorry?"

Claire smooths her fingers over her sundress. "There's really no other way to say it, and there's no way to be sure, but I have a feeling my son would have fallen for you in any time period or any reality you two met in. He's not easy to get along with, but at the same time, he is. And you two just fit together well. It's hard to explain with any other word than soul mates."

She takes a sip from her drink. "But, even if you can't jump or if you didn't want to jump or something in between, you're something more important than your genes. You're family. You taught me that." She smiles, tapping my chest gently.

"Is that why you offered to pull some strings if I decide to go to Harvard?" I ask. "You know that I'm not going to go there just because Blake's going, right?"

The first time Claire offered to help me get into one of the best schools in the nation through her connections, including those in the Time Traveler Association, which spans the world and is like a family, I was skeptical of it. Taking help and getting in based on anything other than my own merit felt a little... wrong.

But then I thought about how many other people, how many white people, do it. How many students get in because their parents give backdoor donations or because of legacy status or for any number of other reasons not based on merit?

"Like I just said, even if you can't time travel, you're still family to me." She shrugs. "And, to me, helping you is about seeing the potential in you, Andre, not about what you can or cannot do for me. Although, you being one of us is a perk, I won't deny that."

"You don't need to, Mrs. McIntyre. Like you said, I'm not stupid." I smile.

"Oh, please. You're family now, and we've been through so much together. This is the last time I'll ask. Call me Claire. Please. I insist."

Mrs. McIntyre—Claire—stands, gliding over to a locked area of the bookshelf. Pulling her key ring out with her back to me, she speaks. "If you're so smart, then why do you think I called you in here?"

I try to peer around her body to see what she's looking at. Curiosity almost makes me stand and walk over, but I stay seated. Something electric in the air tells me that I'll want to be seated.

"I'm guessing to give me some motherly talk about college. You know my biological mother has already given me that, right?"

"Oh, trust me, I know my place with Jennifer. I wouldn't dare cross her."

"You and my mom are on a first-name basis, huh?"

"You're dating my son. And my son is dating hers. What, do you think we'd be enemies?"

I debate telling her how much my mom hated her and Blake when we first started dating, but when Claire turns with a leather-bound book in her hand, any thought about telling her that is replaced with curiosity.

Claire stays quiet, looking at the book. She runs her smooth hands over the cover, slowly walking over and sitting back next to me. The lightness in the room is gone, and the silence is so deafening that the sounds outside of children and music cease to exist.

Finally, after two false starts, she speaks.

"I'm not a person who gives people I care about traditional gifts, Andre. Never have been. And you are no exception," she whispers, passing the book to me. "I hope you can find beauty in the complexity of this gift."

The book feels heavier than I thought it would be. The edges are lined with plastic and have a yellowed tinge to them. The cover is intricately designed in a pattern I've never seen before.

"I don't know how to explain it, but it's like whatever's inside of here is old. But it looks new? Like you could buy this book at Target or something," I whisper.

She smiles, crossing one leg over the other. "We call that 'the sense,'" she explains. "Time travelers can tell the age of things just by touching them. There's much that we don't understand about time travel, Andre. You're living proof of that, and so are the half a dozen or so people throughout time who weren't born in a time-traveling family but gained the ability. It's all fascinating, really."

"Is there a place to study it?" I ask, still mesmerized by the book. "A school or something?"

"Would you be interested, if there is? I suppose I could pull some strings for you. Again."

I smirk and finally open the book.

Instantly, the first picture jumps out at me. It's an image of a man with blond hair, smiling into the camera, standing in front of Stanford University.

That hair.

That smile.

That...

"Michael," I whisper. I barely feel Claire touching my shoulder, rubbing it softly.

I flip through the dozens of pages. Photos of him labeled with years and locations fill the book. His and his boyfriend's first apartment in London. The adoption of their kid. Even photos of him back in between my jumps, like him at Stonewall or at some party with his friends on New Year's Eve party in 1969. There must be at least a hundred photos.

"How did you get these?" I ask five minutes later.

I turn to look at Claire, only to see, not the smirk I was expecting, but instead a kind, soft look. One that resonates compassion, like she understands the feeling of weightlessness and joy that I'm experiencing.

"I told you. I don't give normal gifts." She taps the page with two fingers. "For the past ten months, I've been going back in time. Taking photos and chronicling his life for you. The photos tell their own story, but would you like me to tell you what I saw?"

"Please," I whisper without hesitating.

Claire takes a longer sip this time and crosses her legs at the ankles, getting comfortable.

"Let's see. After you left him, he continued to play his music but decided that his real passion was journalism. He went to Stanford to study it. Wrote some pretty important pieces over the next twenty years about gay rights, disability rights, and intersectionality." She turns to the back of the book, where more than a dozen newspaper articles, each with the byline *Michael Gray* highlighted.

"He got married when he was forty-seven, to a man named Patrick, a car salesman, if you would believe it."

I let out a chuckle. "I can believe it." That sounds like him.

I study the pictures, running my fingers over them. The photos fill in the blanks. Michael looks happy in all of these photos. Pictures of his husband opening up his first independent dealership. His daughter's high school graduation. When he was awarded a Pulitzer. Important moments in any person's life.

But there's a question that the photos don't answer. I do a quick mental calculation. How old would he be now? I guess it doesn't matter. It's not like I'm going to see him again, and if he's dead, how will that make me feel? It took me almost four months to get over him. Four months where Blake was the most patient boyfriend I could ask for. Would knowing whether he's dead or alive throw me back in a way I'm not ready for?

It doesn't matter. I need to know.

"Is he alive?" I force the words out before I can retract them.

Claire pauses, studying the ceiling, as if the answer is up there.

"I need to know."

Eventually, she nods.

"Does that mean that he's alive or that you're nodding in agreement?"

"He's alive," she says. "He's still living a happy and full life. He lives in England with his husband."

I breathe out a shaky sigh of relief and feel tears that I didn't know were pooling around my eyes drop like hot wax down my face. My body shakes in an uncontrollable way. It's just…entropy. So much energy. So much emotion coming out.

"Andre," Claire coos. She turns to me, pulling me close, and I fall into her arms, clinging to them for dear life. She strokes my back slowly, rubbing it in a circle. We sit in silence for what feels like minutes. A comfortable, emotional silence.

Eventually, Claire pulls me back and holds me at arm's length.

"I said he's living a full and happy life. Now you need to do the same. That's what he would have wanted. That's what David would have wanted. That's what I want for you. Now you just have to want it for yourself.

"Michael found what he's passionate about. He found what keeps him going, something to live for. Honor the time you two spent together, and what you had, by doing the same."

"Hey, Mom, Isobel is wond—"

I barely have time to turn my head away and clean up my face before Blake barges in. He stops midsentence, looking at me, then at his mom, then at me again, confusion written all over his features. Claire sighs.

"Blake McIntyre. Can't you *ever* knock?"

But Blake ignores her and beelines straight for me. I want to push him away—I *try* to push him away—but he kneels in front of me, his hands grasping mine, with that stupid grin on his face.

"I don't know what has you so upset, but whatever it is, I'll take care of it, okay? You can count on me."

I smile, shoving him softly. "What would make me feel better is if you don't say cheesy things like that ever again."

"As long as you don't cry ever again, then we have a deal." Blake uses his thumb to brush away my tears. He leans up, pressing a kiss under each of my eyes.

And in that moment, right there, I've never felt happier.

"I'll be right out," I promise him. He stays for a moment, as if he wonders whether I'm going to ask him to stay. "Seriously, I'm okay."

Slowly, he stands. "Isobel is wondering where that Harvard mug is that you said you got her."

Claire points in the general direction of the kitchen. "Top shelf."

"You're a blessing in disguise," he praises his mom, kissing her forehead. "Take care of my boyfriend, all right?"

"I have every intention to."

Once Blake is gone, Claire rests her hands on top of mine, keeping me from moving. "There's something else, Andre."

She takes the book back and opens to the final page, where an envelope is taped. Slowly, Claire peels it off and hands it to me.

The envelope is heavy, and I can feel multiple pages inside. I flip the envelope over and see handwriting that isn't like anyone else's. It takes me a moment to remember the chicken scratch.

Michael.

"During one of my last jumps," Claire explains, "he saw me and approached me. Said he'd seen me all the times I came to visit and scolded me for thinking that I was being stealthy." She chuckles. "He made me promise that I'd give that to you the next time I saw you. I tried to tell him I didn't know what he was talking about, but he didn't buy it. He's a clever one, that man."

"That's what makes him a good journalist," I mutter, transfixed by the letter.

"Would you like me to leave you alone so you can read it?" she asks gently.

I hesitate before answering, thinking over the options. Eventually, I shake my head and tape the envelope, carefully, back where it was before.

Claire smiles brightly. She leans forward, pressing a kiss to my cheek, and stands.

"How about we join the party, hmm? Blake will probably come looking for you again if I keep you away from him for too long."

"I agree. Sounds amazing."

I stand, putting the book on the couch. There will be time for that. Time to examine every photo, remember the past, and imagine his future. But for now, I'm going to look forward. Focus on my future. It's what he would have wanted.

And it's what I want.

Dear Andre,

I've started this letter three times, three different ways, so I think I'll just stick with the simple version. Hi.

I hope this reaches you. I hope you're doing well, but most importantly, I hope you've kept your promise of moving on from me and living your best life.

Here's the truth, Dre: it hurt when you left—real bad. But you were right. I loved what we had, but we both had to live our own lives. I hope you can say the same.

I know you're wondering, so here's the short version: I'm okay. I'm living. Hell, I live a great life. I toured the world. I met a great guy. I've had so many amazing jobs. I found a family. I found someone to love.

I hope you did too. I'll always love you. Always. But, and here's the karmic kicker, we're separated by time and space. We met each other at the wrong time in our lives. And that's okay. Because, despite that, we still got to spend time together. Still got to be together.

And I'm so happy, so honored that I got to meet you. But now it's time for you to live your life, to be happy, to do something great, to tell your own story—another story—without me.

And as someone who loves you, who has always loved you and will always love you, I want that for you more than anything.

So keep this letter close, read it whenever you need, but

that's it. No more jumping to see me, no more sulking, which I know you're doing. Move on, live your life, and be great.

Because, for the Andre Cobb I know, that shouldn't be too hard.

I love you, Andre Cobb from Boston. Always and forever,

Michael Gray

PS: That album we listened to the last time you were here? *Journey in Satchidananda* by Alice Coltrane. Give it a listen. I think you'll enjoy it.

ACKNOWLEDGMENTS

There are a lot of people who need to be mentioned in this book, and never enough space to do it. So many people who helped Dre (because you read his story, you're his friend, you can call him that), Michael, and Blake's story become a reality, people who did small acts of kindness and big ones. If anyone is forgotten, I apologize.

First, I'd like to thank my agent, Jim McCarthy. For answering my million emails, jumping on calls, handling one-off emails and texts in all caps. You're more than an agent. You're a friend, a mentor, a therapist, and everything in between. I'm sure I'm trying a new idea for you to approve as you read this.

I also want to make sure to thank Annie Berger, who bought this weird book two years ago, and all I could think to say in my mind was, *Wow, I have no idea why she bought this crazy idea!* Thank you for working with me on what I would consider my most complicated book, to help me see the truth in the story.

I'd also love to thank Cassie Gutman for taking the time to help take this book over the finish line and Michelle Lecuyer for taking the time to break this book and put it back together. Both of you took this book from *meh* to *amazing*, and I am in awe of what you do every day.

I want to thank Beth Oleniczak, who helped get this book in as many hands as possible. And for everyone at Sourcebooks unnamed, you all are truly the real heroes here. Each book you buy, edit, create, and get into the hands of young people? MVPs, y'all are.

In my life, I want to think my boyfriend, Jordan, for spending countless hours plotting, listening to me rant, and helping me through breakthroughs on this and so many other projects. Lana Johnson, Leah Johnson, the boys of the Ferns group chat—Kevin, Ryan, Caleb, Adam—I wouldn't be sane without you all. Tiffany Jackson—you know what you did, and I appreciate you for it. Booksellers, reviewers, bloggers, champions on Twitter and the internet? Thank you too. And my parents, William and Linda, thank you for creating a space for me to be *me*.

But most of all, I want to thank the readers who picked up this book. I want to thank those who gave me a second chance, who helped me learn, who challenged me, called me out, and helped put me back together. I'm still learning. I'm still growing. And I hope, with each book, each story, and each character, I continue to earn a bit of your trust back and never hurt you all again.

After all, yesterday is history, but that doesn't mean we can't learn from it, am I right?

Onward,
Kosoko

ABOUT THE AUTHOR

Born and raised in the DC Metro Area, Kosoko Jackson has worked in digital communications for the past five years. He is currently an MFA candidate at Southern New Hampshire University's Mountainview MFA program and has a strange love for indie folk, disaster movies, and odd tea flavors. *Yesterday Is History* is his debut. Visit him at kosokojackson.com.

FIREreads

— S #getbooklit —

Your hub for the hottest young adult books!

Visit us online and sign up for our
newsletter at FIREreads.com

 @sourcebooksfire

 sourcebooksfire

 firereads.tumblr.com